GW00692149

Coming soon…

Me, my bicycle and I: Part Two: Middle East and Asia
Me, my bicycle and I: Part Three: South-South-East Asia
Me, my bicycle and I: Around Ireland
Me, my bicycle and I: Around Morocco

ME,
My bicycle
and I:

PART ONE:
THROUGH EUROPE

F. M.

PARTRIDGE

To order additional copies of this book, contact
Partridge India
000 800 919 0634 (Call Free)
+91 000 80091 90634 (Outside India)
orders.india@partridgepublishing.com

www.partridgepublishing.com/india

I know where I was. There is enough information here for you to find out too.

Always let the water flow.

CONTENTS

SYNOPSIS

I had the idea to travel with a bicycle and a tent.
I had the idea, I was not influenced, I was not inspired.
From what you may or may not read, this may sound like an ordinary travel session, but there was no thought about it; it was a get-up-and-go attitude.

I knew where I would be starting, but I did not know where I would be finishing. I wasn't thinking short-term. It should be relatively low cost seeing as I already have two of the bigger costs when travelling. The bicycle being the transport and the tent, the accommodation. What else would a traveller need? Well, what does a human need? Food, shelter, clothing, and water. I have these necessities, though two will need to be replenished when required.

I was not equipped with any fancy gear. The tent that I bought was for around about ten pounds sterling. When I was purchasing the tent, I didn't really think about the negative weather, I really should have checked the parameters. I was sold on 'waterproof.'

This is the beginning of my travel session to one of the edges of Europe. What happens after is beyond.

ACKNOWLEDGEMENTS

The person who sold me their Giant Mountain Bicycle. The person who donated a 'survival kit,' including forty-five-litre backpack.

The eBay user who sold the festival tent.

All of the people I met on the road and many more people.

NETHERLANDS

Back to cycling on Saturday evening, I left Amsterdam, and it was a dripping downpour, the clouds having opened for a torrential storm. It was not miserable to say the least. There was a humid temperature about the city. It was enjoyable, mostly due to the waterproof layers that I had hopingly packed. Being from the North of Ireland, you can never be too sure when there would be rain; it'd be best to be prepared or at least pack a waterproof layer as there would be the inevitable rainfall wherever you go. This is not limited to Ireland.

The city I was aiming for was Utrecht. This took some length of time to reach. First night and all, I didn't want to be pushing myself too hard. I had come across a campsite not too far outside the city. Well, according to the paper road map of Europe that I was using, it was one finger away.

Before this, I was cycling through three small villages right in the middle of nowhere. Well, they had to be somewhere. I can honestly say that I can't remember the names of these villages or the cycle route that I had taken; therefore, these small villages have eluded me, and I am happy about that. I would not be able to remember everything.

It must have been about four o'clock in the morning. I was passing a watering hole in the middle of the fields I was cycling through. A few characters appeared to stumble out of the watering hole. They must have been celebrating their World Cup victory over Costa Rica. They stopped me, and I stopped for a wee break and a chat. I had no idea where I was, apart from being on the road to Utrecht, a place I had only heard about. I could see this on the map, and I was following a cycle sign towards the city from Amsterdam. We chanted and cheered after their victory.

'Are you coming with us?' they asked. I responded with a no as I was too tired to even think about heading off track, too exhausted from the cycling that had been done. I was in need of a bed, and well, I could have hustled a bed out of the situation. I digressed; I was lacking in energy, though they seemed to have plenty. Saying that, the ratio wasn't great; anything could have happened had I gone with them.

As I was getting ready to leave, one of the people asked me to put out my hand. I complied. They dropped in a wee can of water. *Good person*, I thought. *Not often are you given a can of water in the middle of nowhere or even in general for that matter. This will help me progress.*

Now I did not open this can on the spot; I was saving that for a hot summer's day. Once you have opened a can, you should finish the contents in one sitting or there would be the inevitable waste and that is barbaric. I was not ready for that yet. Another occasion would arise when this can of thirst-quenching water could be utilised and enjoyed. I awaited this time patiently; tonight was not that night. I had a bottle.

After the friendly ordeal, I continued cycling east. I came across a campsite which must have been outside Utrecht and set up camp for the night. I had a great sleep, five of five. Pity the tent that I had bought was not completely waterproof. Note to self and others, a tent you buy for ten pounds sterling is a tent that is not going to be completely waterproof. It was sold as a festival tent. I wondered what that could be. I assumed the best. I jest. The tent that I purchased would be used for the duration of a festival, not long term. This was my accommodation, and I didn't plan on changing that. If it rained, I would have to find alternative accommodation.

I arrived into Utrecht that afternoon. The first thing I noticed was that it was one long street, or from the perspective that I had arrived, all the commodities were placed on this one street. As I was picking up breakfast and general supplies for the day ahead, I got speaking to two local people who were doing a spot of grocery shopping. I began speaking to them to find out general information about the small city. They were a good group of people. They even invited me back to their accommodation for a bite to eat and a flask of water. They even put music onto a memory card as I had no music on my tablet. They were both shocked that I was travelling without music. I, on the other hand, had a tablet loaded with music stolen from me in the capital, which was a pity; but surely, these things happen if you are not careful, especially in a hostel. And I guess I was not careful.

I remembered it well. I went out for a shower and had left the tablet under my pillow; it was a quick shower. When I returned, it was gone, and so were the two who were in the room. There were opportunists everywhere. I knew the nationality of the two responsible, but I thought it would be offensive to mention as a small minority already have a bad reputation for selling various goods late at night when revellers are having an enjoyable time. I was happy to cycle onwards without music in between my ears.

When I left and put the earphones in, I realised that we did not have similar tastes in music. And I was basically back to listening to myself. I was not ready for the new music that was cursing through my ears. Of all the gigabytes, it just wasn't for me.

That night, it began to flood down from the heavens because, philosophically, that was where the rain came from. It was too wet to camp, and I didn't want a repeat of the night before, where I would be soaking from the torrential rain that was blasted down on me and my tent. I was tired, and I needed a place to sleep that night in a room with four walls and a roof, the best kind.

Seventeen euros and fifty cents was the best price that I could secure at such short notice, and this was without having a smartphone, where you can find accommodation to suit your requirements and budget super easily. Unlock your phone, open the application, and put in your limits— easy, little to no thought required.

The accommodation would do for the night, but I would have rather slept the night for free. If the bad weather prevailed, I would have to make or find alternative arrangements. This was how it would be from now on. This was unexpected, but you do deal with a problem when it arises. And sometimes the solution was easier than the problem, though the problem I had found here was accommodation in the bad weather. At this stage in the Netherlands, the easiest option would be to find paid accommodation. But several countries later, in Greece, I realised something about camping in the bad weather. Until then, I'd survive through camping and alternative accommodation.

Having to pay to sleep somewhere in a foreign city when you have not organised accommodation beforehand is normal, though in this day and age there are free services to help those who need a place to stay if they are travelling. I didn't think the homeless were aware, though—like me—they may not have access to Internet connectivity to organise. This time, I had not taken advantage of such services as I didn't have the time or the Internet connectivity to arrange such a commodity; plus, I was usually only in a place for the day. Therefore, I would have to plan. I didn't plan on planning anything in terms of accommodation. I had been organised for the past twenty-three years; it was time to let the imaginary hair down, time to release, time to enjoy. Plus, I didn't know when I would be arriving or how long I would be staying; and again, that sounded too organised. I really didn't want that.

I had a tent, therefore accommodation. This was carried on the back, with the shoulders taking the brunt of the load. I carried that with me at all times for this travel session. A paper map and minimal work would do me.

For one night in a random city, I supposed the cost there would be reasonable; this was a Sunday evening. I had expected it to be cheaper, but this was the hostel that I came across. In my opinion, it was wasted money as you only received a bed for the duration of half a night, depending on when you arrived; and then you were out on the street the next morning or, if they were nice enough, the afternoon, with maybe a continental breakfast thrown in for good measure. Now this was when you arrived as an unexpected traveller late at night, looking for a room. It was what it was at short notice, and when day was progressing into night and the weather was not improving, you took what you got or maybe returned after a cycle, scoping out the place to see what else is available.

The hostel was a decent one. It was called Stone Hostel. I found this a funny name for a hostel; the reason was unknown. It was maybe because you throw a stone, not a hostel. The dormitory room had eight beds, and mine was in the corner.

I went into the room, unloaded my backpacks, and spoke to a few who were there. One asked if I wanted to go for a jar of water; again, I was too exhausted and would rather unwind with a flask of water after a long day of cycling and travelling in the rain. I went to the bathroom to use the facilities. When I returned to the room to get ready for sleep, the lights were turned off. I opened the door and walked to the bed.

In my peripheral vision, I could see a figure in the light. As I passed one of the upper bunk beds, one of the lights was on and I heard a high-pitched voice from the darkness. I laughed and went to bed. That was weird— well, not really, another opportunist. You do hear about how creepy some European hostels can be. Hostels invited people from all walks of life; the vibrations sent out rang out to everyone. Which is not necessarily a good thing...

Luckily, my bed was in the corner of the room on the second bunk. I found it funny at the same time as you hear about many strange and weird occurrences happening in hostels, and well, this was my first strange experience thus far. Hostels can be weird, not the building itself but some of the people that they can attract. I was not a fan of hostels per se. They were all right, and they did serve a purpose. It would be best to be careful about your personal belongings and things that you hold important (e.g. passport). It could be easier that way.

That morning, I awoke and dilly-dallied for about an hour before making the move from a comfortable reclined position to back outside to the concrete environment. At that time, I was able to look at the map and to continue on a route that would take me farther as I travelled with a bicycle, final destination unknown. For now, I cycled. I was only in my first country in Europe, and I didn't know what I envisioned. I knew I would see the sun soon.

Cycling on the front suspension mountain bicycle, I saw a cycle sign for Arnhem, which would be another twenty kilometres away. From what I remembered, there were a few graveyards in between where all the graves were cemented shut. Needless to say, I had not planned on digging any up. But why would they feel the need to shut them closed? One example would be to stop animals from digging up the graves, and I am sure you could think of a few yourselves, fairly self-explanatory if you thought about it. I gave an example, not the reason.

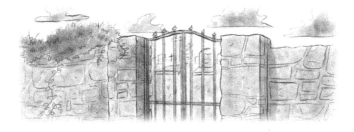

Arnhem was a small town with many bridges and churches scattered throughout and also a wide variety of ethnicities walking about the streets, and I was one of them on a bicycle. I cycled through the town with not much to be absorbing in. Now it was time to find accommodation for the night. A campsite would be preferable, but I would happily take a hostel or a bed somewhere.

I came across a one-star hotel, and I enquired about the price. It would be thirty euros for a night without breakfast. I laughed and continued onwards. Thirty euros for one night at a hotel? I could invest that money in something worthy. They advised of a Stay OK Hostel not far from the hotel. I followed the directions, but I got lost along the way, and I was near sure I was on my way out of Arnhem.

I stopped and asked a person at the side of the road for directions. They were very friendly. As we got talking, they had told me they were working in the hospital right next to us. I was invited into their office, and I was given several jugs of water. Was I going to be staying here this evening? I really had no idea what was happening, but I was out of the bad weather, which I was happy about. After the jugs of water, they were able to show me to a sports ground where I was able to pitch my tent for the night. Very helpful they were.

That morning, I awoke to the sound of rain battering the tent; water was dripping in through the single thin layer of material. I was beginning to get wet. I supposed it was time to get up, get out, dismantle the tent, and pack my backpacks. I then continued towards the direction of the hospital to have breakfast and use the free Wi-Fi. The day continued, raining all day. It wasn't even that miserable. All types of weathers can be enjoyable if you are prepared. I think this depends on the chosen attire. If you had efficient clothing for different weathers, you were going to have a good time.

As I was eating breakfast, the person I met last night came over and sat down as they had just finished their night shift. I was shown to the shower facilities, but I was not able to have a ward bed for the night, which was understandable. I had a tent; this was my accommodation that would be utilised throughout this travel session. This tent, had camped in twenty different countries which spanned three continents. It served its purpose well.

I finished my breakfast, which consisted of at least a banana and bread. I looked out the window of the foyer, and the weather had not shifted. I was content. The person and I decided to go for a drive around the municipality and surrounding area. One of the places we stopped at was a graveyard. And we looked at various monuments and bridges throughout the city. The graveyard was not a nationalist one, I believe.

Before I knew it, it was six o'clock in the evening. It was time to make tracks from Arnhem and head towards the next place on the map, which would be Nijmegen. I had several directions that I could choose—east, north, south. I wouldn't be going back west anytime soon.

It rained constantly, though luckily I had packed a completely waterproof layer, which would be very important. The rain was not really an issue.

Upon entering the municipality of Nijmegen, there was a large bridge that connected the south to the north, crossing over a large river, Waal. I continued straight into the heart of Nijmegen. On the high street, I cycled past a place called Shamrock's Irish Bar. It was still raining buckets at this stage. I decided to head into the watering hole to keep out of the bad weather and to get a jar of water; plus, the World Cup quarter finals were on, Brazil versus Germany. I arrived into the watering hole forty minutes into the game. Already, the score was four goals to Germany. I was shocked to see the home side receive such a thrashing, and it wasn't even half-time. I was also delighted. The match ended with seven goals to Germany, one to Brazil.

As the watering hole was closing up, I got speaking to some of the locals and the bartender. They had mentioned an orange march which was starting on Monday, the fourteenth of July, and said that I should stay for it. I said that I would not be staying as I did not like the sound of it. If I were to choose a coloured theme for a march to attend, it would not be orange. I was only travelling through. I would not stay in Nijmegen for any longer than a night. I would only end up spending some money there—money which would be better utilised elsewhere.

The local people were kind enough to let me pitch my tent in the back of their garden, which was handy considering there were not many hostels or campsites near the vicinity that were visible late at night, though I didn't really look. Silly to say, but if I had a connected mobile phone, this would be easy or easier at least. The advantage of not having a connected device on the go is that there can be greater interaction with the locals who know the craic, though you can pay for interaction. The garden seemed secure enough. Plus, if someone gave you authority to camp on their plot, then it was fair game. Be respectful, or if the vibrations were not too positive, do what you feel was right for you.

That morning, I awoke and ate my breakfast, which consisted of two bacon rashers, bread made by the locals, and a jug of water. I also used the Wi-Fi before departing. After I had left, about thirty minutes later, I had realised I no longer had my large backpack with me. How on earth could I have forgotten that? This was basically my home or even, contained my home. I must have gotten preoccupied with dismantling the tent in the rain, even though I would have put the tent back into the backpack. I was puzzled.

I had left the house not long ago, and well, I had no idea where I had cycled to, to retrace my steps. I was moving on the bicycle, not paying attention. I had left my passport and everything at the house. Was this the end? Or was this just the beginning? Would everything still be there when and if I returned? Or was it too early to tell? These were the sorts of questions that I pondered while I was trying to retrace my steps on such a miserable day. It was a miserable day only because I couldn't get started when I had departed. I would have to wait until I contacted the tenants or miraculously remembered where the house was. This did not seem likely.

There was a fairly advanced device inside the backpack that could be used to convert the thermal energy from a fire into electrical charge to charge USB devices such as phones and tablets. It was not a cheap piece of kit. One thing that was said to me was to not lose it or break it. It may be in two pieces, but I assumed it still worked. The reason I did not know was that the weather conditions had not been great.

I knew I should have gone south from the day I had started, but I thought that route would have been too hot. I was glad I had taken this route as, to me, this was the complete unknown. Had I gone south, I would have been basically following the coast; and well, that can be predictable. I didn't want predictable. The coast seemed fairly straightforward—follow the road and go on your way to your destination.

I was beginning to get slightly agitated. I backtracked and backtracked again and again, but I wasn't finding the street where I had left my belongings. Where were my belongings? Would they still be there? Would I find the house? I would say that luck was not on my side, but I didn't believe in that superstition. If it was meant to be, then it would be.

I found a cafe, ordered a jug of water, and used the customer Wi-Fi to send an email to the tenant of the house. I waited for a reply, drank more water, and then had another jug. When I was charging my tablet, I noticed paper maps of Nijmegen. I was able to see and locate where I had spent the night. With a trusted pencil, I was able to mark out a location on the map with an X.

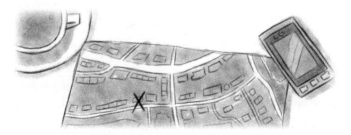

I arrived to the house, and relief hit me when my backpack was still there.

I left Nijmegen and headed for Germany. Nijmegen was only fifteen kilometres from the German border. Once again, I found myself cycling the distance in the rain. It was not a bother though. Rain gives this person energy; it is water after all.

GERMANY

The first noticeable difference between the Netherlands and Germany that I experienced was that there was much more rain, hills, and vegetation when I crossed the border. Netherlands was a very boring country to cycle in, but everything was flat; therefore, distance can be covered at pace. It took me three days to go through it, and that was coasting along, not pushing myself too much. I had broken into country number two, a country that I had never visited before.

The first point of interest I came across was the town of Kleve, which consisted of several statues of eagles on top of podiums. They were at the top of a garden area with a forest surrounding. The podiums were as high as the deciduous trees that towered the eagles, if not taller. It was some sight to look at.

There was a sense of darkness about the area and forest and not because it had been raining all day. Kleve was a small municipality steeped in history. Some of this evidence was found in the stonework in the various castle-like structures. It was a wet day, and this wee town was interesting enough.

Before I knew it, it was time for sleep; and I needed shelter, a bed, and a jug of water. Too wet to pitch a tent for the night, I had to find alternative accommodation. When I was cycling and walking through the small town, I came across a map at the side of the road and located all the town's amenities. There was a *Jungerbehaus*, which I believed to mean 'youth hostel.' I followed the map and found what I was looking for. I have since been corrected; Jugenherberge. But I still found what I was looking for!

The place reminded me of Cabra Towers in Newcastle, County Down, Ireland. There was even a pong in the air. The cashier was German, funnily enough, and they could not really understand english, though this was Germany. In the end, it would be twenty euros for the night, plus an extra four euros for a hostelling card, which I may never actually use as I had not been prebooking any hostels and had not really planned on staying in them. However, if I stayed with the same hostelling company more than six times, I would receive a free bed. It wasn't really worth it, spending money to save money. This one seemed well out of the way from the amenities. The next time I came across one of the hostels was in Dubai, United Arab Emirates, country number fourteen. I am getting ahead of myself.

I was shown to my room. I ended up being the only one to stay there that night. Thank the higher power. I had plenty of items to dry. I had to sort out my clothing, dry my tent, and make plenty of noise throughout the night. I didn't have much time to get everything dried as I was busy and had a tight time frame, and I needed sleep. Not to worry, as I would get adequate sleep. By morning, everything was dry, and I had made much noise.

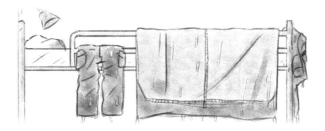

Now it was time to repack and head into the foyer for breakfast. There was no Wi-Fi at the hostel, which was a joke. And the back-up option of the television was not working either. Technical difficulties much? Unfortunately, I was unable to watch the Netherlands versus Argentina quarter final. Argentina won. It was only football. At least with the World Cup, there is a general interest across the globe as there are international teams competing on a football field for the famous fabricated golden trophy.

Breakfast was decent. I couldn't really fault it—cereal with a dash of milk, a few pieces of toast, some type of meat (possibly ham), cheese, cucumber, and juice. I ate until I was content and probably took a few items for the rest of the day too.

That day was my birthday. I left the hostel that morning at around ten o'clock in search of the next town. The clouds in the sky were beginning to shift. It was too hot when midday approached, though it usually is around this time. I was on the way farther east. I came across a place called Wunderland Kalkar. It was in the middle of nowhere. In the same place I was. *What am I doing here? Oh wait, following a road to the next town.*

As it was my birthday, I was looking for something *fun* to do. I decided to follow the signs for a few kilometres, and as I was approaching, I could see the Wunderland in the distance. I turned around on the road as it was not the theme park that I had imagined. I was expecting to see large roller coasters in the distance and a few other machines but was severely disappointed, so I turned back around on the road I was following. It was like that place that was opposite the Park Centre in Belfast—Dreamland, which was there once upon a time.

It was very, very hot, and I needed water. I opened the tablet and used the downloaded offline German language pack to translate 'Can I have some water, please?' When translated using Google Translate, it was 'Kahn ich habe estow wasser, bitte?' Luckily, there was a Lidl around the corner from where I was, and I did not have to interact with the German people.

I spent eighteen cents for a one-and-a-half-litre bottle. Unfortunately, once I left the supermarket, I noticed it was sparkling water, which was not a favourite. I still drank it, but I was not impressed. It was a taste that I had not acquired, nor did I intend to. It was rank, rotten and rough on the tongue, though the day is still early.

I continued forth, and I began to notice a red patch forming on my left arm and was kind of shocked as I wondered where the rash had possibly come from. I quickly got over it and continued. But I was still unsure what it was.

I had planned to follow the river Rhine right down to Cologne. This did not prove successful as there were no cycle paths right beside the river; they had ended for now. It reminded me of the river Lagan back home, where there are cycle paths beside the river; then all of a sudden, they come to an abrupt end, leading you nowhere really.

Germany really was different compared with the other countries that I had visited. It was mostly the nature and how vibrant it was in the summer. It really was something else.

I decided to cross the river Rhine and follow signs to the nearest town, Rees. There was not much there, just several churches and a sculpture museum which I randomly came across. It was fun to walk about and look at the large structures. I set off on the path and cycled for Wesel.

Cycling in the sun with a short-sleeved T-shirt was probably not the wisest decision. I did not think about picking up sun cream because I was not on a holiday; and well, on a holiday, you wear sun cream.

Water is a necessity which constantly needs replenishing as you cycle, as you do get thirsty. I would need to find a reasonable supply soon.

As I was cycling, the Rhine was on my right. I must have cycled a good number of kilometres before taking a break and resting. As I was cycling, I came across a person who was sleeping on a bench. They did not look homeless, I approached them to see if they were all right and to not get sunburnt like I had. We got speaking, and they were learning to speak english. We were able to converse, and they may have learnt a thing or two.

I did not know how we got onto the topic of birthdays, but it was said that it was my birthday. They asked if I would like to go for a jar of water in the blistering heat. I was in no hurry. They told me to continue cycling onwards until I reached a mural, and they had said they would meet me there in their car. We went for a drink in Wesel in a nice watering hole and restaurant where several could see the river Rhine flowing past.

We parted ways after our jars of water, and I continued to cycle. They had mentioned about a ferry that was crossing the river and that it only crossed on Friday and Saturday. When I got to the boat depot, there were many people waiting. I assumed the person I met did not know all the days of the week, or maybe it was some form of trickery.

After I had crossed the river to continue cycling, I came across a camping ground, thirty euros for a night for one person and one tent. 'No thank you. I will find another place to camp, thank you very much.'

I continued to cycle until about eleven or twelve o'clock at night, racking up the kilometres as I glided. I came across a McDonald's in the middle of nowhere, Rheinberg. At the McDonald's, I could hear a number of thick english accents. It was very random, but once I heard the accents, I knew there would be accommodation nearby.

We all ate our food and went back to a hotel collectively. Fifty euros was the cost. No thank you. 'Is there anywhere I can camp out the back?' I asked the owner.

'Yes,' they replied.

I headed around to the back of the hotel, where there was a garden. I set up camp. I had an enjoyable sleep after a long day of cycling. It was my first birthday on my own, and I had had quite an eventful day. The highlight was probably the crematorium I had went into during the midday heat to evade the sun. There was a good bunch of people there. They probably thought I was a friend of the deceased. Before that, I was speaking to a German, and I asked for direction. I got my answer. As they were leaving, I said to them, 'Nein schweiß.' They were not happy about that. 'No sweat,' and away I went.

Happy birthday to me. If only I was still twenty-three. However, this does not matter when free.

That morning, I awoke just before nine o'clock to disassemble my tent and leave Rheinberg. Next stop would be Cologne. I wanted to be in the city for the World Cup final. The capital, Berlin, was too far north-east to even think about. I was too far north-west of Germany to begin making tracks up, nor would I be paying for a train. As I cycled without hesitation, I knew that I would have to cover much ground to reach the destination.

Many places along the way that I began to detest included Düsseldorf and Duisburg, two industrial towns that I had to cycle through to continue on the path. With the heat that was encapsulating my body and the numerous industrial plants I had cycled through, it was time to find some water. Several hours passed, and I was in Cologne. As I entered the city, there was much roadwork happening towards the central station. It was handy as I had one side of the road all to myself.

It was getting dark, so I began to look out for hostels as it can be hard to find a place to camp free from people in the city or where you did not have to get up at the crack of dawn. The first one on the edge of the city was full to the brim apparently, but the person there working reception was able to give me a selection of leaflets which were able to guide me towards accommodation. They had also mentioned about wild camping along the Rhine. This was the first time I had come across the expression 'wild camping' as, back home, we call it camping. It was probably because there were various campsites scattered throughout the country, and I didn't think it was the norm to be camping without a shower here; that is an assumption.

Wild camping sounded like too much for a Friday night. I wanted a bed indoors, preferably free, which was not looking likely on a Friday night. A Friday night is the end of the traditional work-week; this can be special for those people who work within this timeframe, which is the norm. My point is, Friday usually has events and functions; therefore, it was looking like I would have to find accommodation to take advantage of this potential offering.

As I travelled forwards in search of the city centre, I was amazed at what I could see, a proper German city. Considering I had been cycling through small municipalities, this was my first real German experience. I found one of the hostels from the leaflets. It was right around the corner from the central station. There was a large alien-like spaceship right in the centre. This structure was the Cologne Cathedral. I went into the hostel to enquire about the price of a bed—twenty-four euros and fifty cents. I told the attendant I would think about it.

Several minutes passed. A hosteller came out to get fresh air. 'Oi, mate, are you stayin' here tonight? Few of us are heading to some techno club,' they said in a thick english accent. I was near sick in my mouth but was attracted to what they had said.

After a few minutes of convincing, I got a room. I had a shower, put on fresh clothes, and headed out later that night. Two trains later, we arrived at the techno club under a bridge. The cost of a ticket was not extortionate. I didn't fancy waiting in the queue; therefore, I hopped over the fence and into the music. Luckily, there were no bouncers at the other side. They might have been working the doors as, out the back, it wasn't exactly thriving yet. The rest continued to wait until they were released into the club, and I met them there. This took them about an hour while I absorbed the atmosphere, culture, and music, which were similar to events in Belfast—events that did not attract the average human – Think Annaghtek.

The next day, I awoke in an apartment. I thought I may have had too many jars of water the previous night or maybe the right amount. I checked the time, and it was eleven o'clock in the morning. Oh, I better get back to the hostel to check out. I had no idea how to get back. I was given directions to the train station from the people at the apartment; this proved useless as the trains were not really operating at this time, or that was what I thought.

'Taxi!' I shouted in the street.

'How much?' I said to the driver.

'Ten euros', they replied.

'No thank you,' I replied.

The next taxi I didn't even bother to ask; it would be what it was. In I bounced. The taxi driver did a good job; I felt like they were my chauffeur because they were driving me to the destination that I needed to go. It was good to have someone else do the work.

I arrived at the hostel, quickly had a shower, packed up my backpacks, and headed down the stairs. At the reception, I asked for a locker to store my belongings— freedom. That day, I was able to enjoy the finer sides of Cologne without the restrictions of a backpack, which was holding me back. This became fairly evident throughout my travels when I arrived to the big cities. Tehran, Iran was one of these places where I began to feel the force of the backpack. It can be awkward at times having this massive backpack on my shoulders not because of the weight per se but because my mind was always thinking about it; it contained some of the most important documents that I would need. If I lost the backpack, well, that would be another story. Nearing the end of the travelling session, I did lose something; it was not a passport. That was lost in India on the twenty-ninth day of a thirty-day visa. But I did lose something very important, something that cannot be replaced. For now though, I was in Cologne, Germany.

The first stop was to check out the Cologne Cathedral in the natural light. This was something else. The stonework, the height, the size, and the surrounding area was almost mind blowing as it was foreign to this traveller. It was such a great structure surrounded by the hustle and bustle of the city. Out of nowhere stood one of the largest cathedrals I had ever seen, not that this was important; it was memorable. Looking up at the structure from the ground and the irregular shapes of the stonework was remarkable and definitely worth the visit. Luckily, I happened to just come across it while cycling. No return direct flight for me.

I set off on my bicycle again, heading around the city. In the distance, I could see a large tower shadowing the other buildings. Great, something to follow unlike the roads and signs that I had previously been following.

Though I was still following roads, I could see that the distance to the radio tower was considerably getting closer, and my destination was within grasp. While cycling the roads, you had no real indication of how close you were.

The tower was in front of me, and I could see all its magnificence. At the time, there was no way of getting to the top. The base of the tower was in the local park. As I progressed through the park, I could see two gazebos with what looked like a sound system. I headed over to the happening and began to speak with the locals. They offered me food and jars of water.

As the day progressed into the evening, a game of football was played. That night, there was a party where all the guests were also having jars of water and cups. It was a water party, maybe for someone's birthday, but I didn't quite know who. I enjoyed myself and went back to the hostel lifted as I had absorbed in some of their culture, which was similar to various cities across the globe. I had slept at the happening on Saturday night, which was handy as I didn't have to pay for a second night at the hostel. I was saving money.

Money was a funny one. You work two jobs before leaving and take advantage of the zero-interest student overdraft as you travel; well, that was what I had done. The student overdraft was extended to near the maximum, enough to play with for a year, mostly transfers to a normal, everyday account. Spoiler alert, they cut off the overdraft in Asia; I am near sure, it wasn't that eventful. Losing a bank card in Thailand was more eventful.

This day was the World Cup final. I arrived back to the hostel and sneakily headed into the luggage room to grab a change of clothing and toiletries to have a wash. Done, clean and ready for potential action. It would be a biggish night as Germany played Argentina in the World Cup final.

I went into the foyer of the hostel to use the free Wi-Fi and bumped into the english person from Friday night. There were a few people there who were going to see the match on a big screen in one of the parks. We headed off, not really knowing where we were going, but we could see the masses of people all heading in one direction—best to follow. Next thing I knew, we were at the park from the previous day. The tower still baffled me; they should have kept the restaurant at the top open. I would have happily ordered a jar of water to gaze out the window or went up for a quick walk around the perimeter, maybe pretending I was a waiter for those brief minutes for the craic; I did have a black shirt.

We found the football grounds where they were showing the World Cup final. It was funny to watch the people shouting and screaming at every chance. It was a weird and enjoyable experience. Time passed, and the home side got their goal. It was on the twenty-third minute of extra time. The place then erupted. It was lit up like a fire doused in petrol. It was funny to watch all the spectators (apart from the Argentines) celebrate the goal. 'Deutschland, Deutschland, Deutschland!' they chanted.

Everyone took to the street for a party. All the Germans were in a good mood. It was a great experience to be part of; they were all running about the streets buck wild—well, the majority were. There was an ambulance trying to get through the mass of people. Some people got in the way of the ambulance, and this turned the happy time into something else. Fists began to be thrown in all directions. The people who tried to block the ambulance obviously didn't understand how important ambulances are and received what they deserved; there was no organisation, almost chaotic. I removed myself from the scene or at least went into the background.

The next day, I woke up in the middle of a bank which had been closed. It was more of a cash machine room, but I slept there that night, saved me from having to pay for the hostel; plus, it was very convenient at the time. That night, I had my replacement tablet stolen. Even at the hostel, I was reluctant to take it with me as I knew how much of a precious tool it had been and could be. It was only a piece of material goodness whose main objective was for communicational purposes. I was sure I would come across another one on my travels.

That day, I awoke to the sound of the clean-up operations. Various machines were cleaning the streets, banners were being removed, and the World Cup was over. Back to work and routines. It was as if they had never won. Their faces returned to their normal looks, not the ecstatic one's from the previous night.

On Monday afternoon after a shower, I went into the foyer of the hostel and got speaking to someone who was at the football match and found out they were cycling too. 'Maybe we could partner up for a while,' I said to them We were going to two different places, but we would both be following the Rhine, so that would be handy. We had both finished with Cologne, so we hopped on our bicycles, picked up supplies as well as extra calories from the local cheeseburgers, and headed for the Rhine.

Neither of us knew exactly where to go, but we found our way there. It was a rather large river after all. We found it and began to head down the river. Why had I never thought about river cycling before? Okay, I had before when I was following the Rhine farther up, but the cycle ways from here continued as far as the river stretched. It was like the German people had invested in leisure for the nationals as well as foreigners. River cycling, it was so simple. Follow the river, minimal hills, easy riding. We must have cycled about thirty kilometres before taking a break and resting while having a flask of water after a fragile start to the day. Good going. Wild camping was completed along the Rhine after several more kilometres. I had always thought it was safer to camp in two for greater security. Two is better than one. One can be dangerous.

Along the riverfront, there were many rocks, stones, pebbles, and debris covering the floor. I decided to clear a space to assemble the tent for the night. During the time spent at the location, a fire was lit, and it was roaring. It served its purpose well by distributing heat, boiling water for a jug of water, and also providing thermal energy needed to charge electronic devices using the special charger I had.

Pity, at the time, all I had was a phone that received no signal outside Ireland and was not Android. Other than a camping utensil, this device could be used for those who are homeless or without power. The user could use thermal energy from a heat source such as fire to charge or even power their devices. It was as if it had been invented in the past, but only now had it come to the present. It was such a simple analogue-to-digital converter, an innovative piece of technology, though there would be an initial cost, a cost some may not be able to afford.

The next day, I awoke to the sound of passers-by and the occasional dog coming over to have a sniff and possibly urinate on the tent; luckily, none came through the single-layered canopy. It was time to get up and hit the road again. A flask was had, and we were golden. That day was like any other, roasting. The reason I started to head east was to try to avoid the sun a little, as had I gone south from the start, I would have burnt to a crisp.

Touring Germany on a front suspension mountain bicycle was great. This was only the second country of a list that could be bigger than my hands. I really had no idea at this stage. I had an idea, but plans can change all of a sudden. We cannot predict the future. Imagine if we could though. You could see the ending before it had happened. It would certainly save you the hassle. But have patience; we will get there.

We had more Rhine cycling and more visual stimulants along the river. We eventually came to a campsite, fifteen euros for two nights with a perfect view of the Rhine from comfortable seats. I thought, people, mainly Germans, actually plan a holiday here. There were a load of camper vans and only one tent on the plot. We had randomly came across it as we were cycling. It was a tranquil spot away from the noise of the German families. All was well, and the water was flowing. We stayed two nights and then went on the road again.

As we progressed up the Rhine, the visual landscape began to change once again into something more beautiful. I never knew there were mountain-type hills in Germany. There were so many castles along the way that were on top of what I would describe as canyons; it was more breathtaking than I had imagined, though I hadn't thought about it previously. I had not even thought about the route I would be taking before I left; I knew I would have time. I didn't know what to expect as I continued farther down the Rhine. When I was younger, I used to think the river Lagan was some spot to cycle, but this was something much more majestic.

That night, we parted ways; it had been a good journey together, but we were cycling at a different pace and out to see different things. Plus, I was drinking most of their water. That night, I found a campsite at a place called Rhens, less than ten euros for the tent. I kind of didn't want to pay for it but I was drained of energy, possibly the sun throughout the day. I decided to call it a night. I read a chapter of a book and headed to bed at eleven o'clock after a scrub and shower.

That morning, I must have left the campsite at about ten o'clock in search of Mainz. All along the Rhine, the river changed from pretty to prettier. It was nice to absorb that which I had never seen before.

Cycling in the heat was bearable, although when you were travelling south-east, what did you expect? You expected the climate to change a little, and well, it had for the better. I expected less rain, though rain can be random.

There was much along the way to view. I stopped at a village for some lunch. It was a small place which consisted of a cafe and a Catholic church, not much really but that depends on your perspective.

One hundred kilometres later, I arrived in Mainz, a street filled with a lot of history and architecture. It was like I had stepped into Germany before the war. All along the way towards the campsite, all I could see were posters for the new McDonald's burger. I did want one but opted for a healthy dinner instead, which consisted of a sandwich and a muffin.

A campsite was found, and it was time to get ready for bed, although the campsite was full of families. There was a family beside me; they had finished their meal and were away from the table. Now was time for me to head over to see what had been untouched. I found a feast. Several minutes had passed, and I could hear a person shouting. I assumed about the food!

I awoke that morning, packed my gear, and headed into the Mainz centre for lunch. I sat in the centre of the square beside the Mainz dome and ate a pizza pretzel which I bought from a vendor. It wasn't even that nice, it was stinkin' but I ate it anyway, too salty for me. I also ate a pear and drank a one and a half litre bottle of Fanta I had bought for eighty-eight cents. And somehow that would cost nearly three times the price back home. As I was eating lunch, I could hear a saxophone player in the distance playing music; plus, the sound of the local market on a Saturday afternoon was buzzing. It was an enjoyable lunchtime experience.

That afternoon, I left for Frankfurt, which was only forty kilometres away according to a signpost, which was handy when it was going the way you wanted to go. Sometimes with the paper road map of Europe, not all the villages and towns were listed, and you had to take a risk and choose a direction. This was the map I had. I didn't plan on changing that—while in Europe.

I saw a person on a BMX at a local skatepark I was passing and I asked if I can have a ride on it. I got off my twenty-six-inch mountain bicycle and hopped onto the twenty-inch BMX. Firstly, I felt like I was a clown on one of those very small bicycles; secondly, I had lost all control over the bicycle and called it a day.

As I cycled up the river Main, I came across a small festival with live music. I heard some ska music, a cross of jazz with punk-like rhythm; this got me to stay there. I had a look around, sampled the tents, and ate some more food. About an hour later, I decided that it would be time to hit the road. As I was about to leave, I decided to stay after coming to the realisation that I could do with staying there and enjoying the randomness of the festival and the atmosphere; plus, it seemed as though there was free camping—well, I did not pay.

I assembled my tent and continued with the festival—decent music, German people, and ice-cold jars of water on tap on a very sunny day. I walked past the tent beside mine, peered in, and saw a group of people sharing cups of water; and for some reason, I didn't feel like having that water. I had a few cups back in Cologne and, well, nothing new there. I saw several different bands ranging from traditional folksy music to heavy metal to ska. As the night progressed, I decided to call it a night as I had had enough of the festival and headed for the tent. It was a repetitive atmosphere.

That morning, I arose from my sleep and began to disassemble my tent. A nice person from the tent beside mine had put my trainers under the canopy to keep them dry as I think there was a little drizzle the night before— sound person. Then I had an ice-cold shower that properly woke me up. I assumed the festival was an independent, which led me to think whether the festival was legal as many people were arguing about the noise from the aircrafts which were passing the nearby villages; plus, a few posters helped me with my conclusion, and I thought the festival may have been a protest, but I could be wrong. In the end, you could say the people were right. They were fighting noise with sound. One could say that there may as well be some sort of productive noise rather than the noise of the planes; at least the festival helped solve that problem but not the visual. Don't look up, I suppose.

On my bicycle I hopped and headed for Frankfurt, only about thirty kilometres away. From about ten kilometres, I could see the city landscape with several large buildings jutting out from the ground. Now I could see why someone described it as the London of Germany. It was the financial district.

When I arrived, it was about eleven thirty in the morning. I came across another large cathedral which I could see from the river that I was following, the Frankfurt Cathedral. Frankfurt Cathedral was large, though not as spectacular as the cathedral in Cologne. Again, it was just a massive structure in the centre of the city popping out of nowhere; again, it was as if the city were built around the structure, which would be different in today's society, I think.

I had passed a hostel earlier upon entry. I asked about the price, and it was thirty euros. At the time, the sun was shining, and the weather was cool. I asked if I could have a shower and if I could store my backpacks for the afternoon; they complied. I really needed a shower after cycling for three hours as the temperature was great though fairly humid.

I headed up the river Main to see if I could find a way out for when I was ready to leave. I found a place called Hanau, and I checked the map; it was closer to the Czech Republic border. I stopped for lunch along the riverfront. As I was cycling, I could see a market across the river, many tents and stalls.

After lunch, I headed over to have a look around, which was mostly clothing, kind of like a jumble sale by the river. The only item I found was a first-generation iPod touch being sold for fifteen euros. I haggled the person down to nine euros, though I was unsure if I wanted to buy the device as the touch did not come with a charging cable. Therefore, I did not know if it worked; and well, neither did they, or so they said. I walked around the market for a wee while, browsing to see what I could find, nothing much.

I made a decision to purchase the device. As I was handing the money over, the vendor decided to ask the next vendor about my money. They conversed and had a laugh and a wee joke between themselves. At this stage, I decided to retreat from the idea of buying the iPod as, to be honest, I had no idea whether the music player worked. It would be as if I was giving the person the money for no good cause if the device did not work, or it was as good as losing the money; therefore, I decided to hold on to my nine euros. That was more than food for the day.

I was happy, and I returned to the hostel to grab my belongings and headed to Hanau along the river Main. I came across a sign that said 'Hanau 9 kilometres or Hanau 11 kilometres'. I opted for the nine-kilometre route, hopped on a boat, and began to cross the river. I continued into Hanau and began cycling once again.

The rain had been stopping and starting throughout the evening. As much as I had wanted it to rain at night, it was fairly heavy; and well, my tent cannot cope with that, but I can. I stopped at a place called Seligenstadt. I found a large tree to camp under and decided to put up my tent for the night. Luckily, I had torches, so erecting in the dark was not a problem. As I lay in the tent, I could feel large droplets of water coming through and soaking my sleeping bag. It was time to leave and find another place to camp. I moved my tent about ten metres to the left, closer to a large wall and under a small tree.

The rain fizzled out eventually, and I was able to sleep until about eight o'clock in the morning—three of five for that sleep. It was time to get up. There was a person passing who asked if I would like a jug of water as they did not live far away. I complied; after the night I had, a jug of water sounded powerful.

We headed off into the small village of Seligenstadt, which looked like it had been there for many, many years. When we approached the house, it reminded me of a place close to home; granda's garage – big wooden doors, few holes and a latch. We entered. I set the bicycle up against the wall. *Hopefully, no one will steal it*, I thought. We headed in for the jug of water. I was even offered a shower, which was taken at the drop of a hat. Best shower I have had thus far. The house inside was modern with the original support beams on show with all the latest white goods. The person gave me their address and said they would like a postcard from Prague. I hope I can comply.

What an afternoon I have had. After leaving Seligenstadt, I continued on up the river Main until I reached a place called Aschaffenburg, which had a castle. I walked up a steep incline, had a look around, and headed off. A castle was the highlight. As I was cycling, I saw a road sign for Würzburg, a place that I would be going through to reach the Czech Republic. I followed the sign as I wanted to get off the river and try to progress as quickly as I could for no reason other than to make distance and to break into the third country. Germany had been decent, mostly visually.

Any journey that began uphill was one that I didn't want to be part of, only if necessary—and well, this was not. I climbed to the top of a hill which was close to a Lidl and then all the way down; then there was another hill and another, and it would only be another sixty kilometres after that, not too bad. Just follow the signs to reach your destination. I called into a tourist shop as I needed to see where exactly I was going as there was a sign for the motorway, and well, I know I cannot cycle there; it would be the autobahn. They had informed me to go back the way I had come. Back up these hills again then.

After a few kilometres, I decided to make a self-directed decision and returned to where I was that morning, which was a big downer. I had enough for one day. It was not a journey for half-flat tyres and about twenty kilograms excess on the back of myself. Plus, I was not a car. Now to continue up one more hill and back to more river cycling.

I was back to where I started in the morning. As I sat beside the river, I asked someone if they knew of a *campingplatz*. They directed me to the castle, over there somewhere apparently. A heron just flew past, which reminded me of the dead heron I had seen at the side of the road. What was it doing there? I thought they were water birds. Poor thing. Onto the next life, I suppose.

Also, as I sat there, I thought about all the junk food I had eaten throughout that day. I was almost saddened at this thought as it really went to show that you must have a correct diet to perform when travelling with bicycle and in general, especially if you wanted optimal performance. Learn from your mistakes and all that. Today I felt like a pig; that was what I was, a fat pig. *Still, as I sat here, I hear the wind. Seems like it is going to be a long night.*

On the road again. I continued to cycle and came across a campsite about twenty kilometres away. Oh, the relief to find a safe place to camp for the night. I was going to camp at a park not far from the campsite but thought differently as there was a sign saying 'No Camping' and I didn't want to get fined at this stage or even be asked to move on throughout the night. It was the cost of the campsite versus the cost of the fine; still, I was tempted.

I arrived after dark; putting up the tent was not a problem. I did ask at reception beforehand in case it was seen as rude to pick a spot and erect. The campsite had advertised that the reception closed after ten o'clock. It was well into the night by then, which meant that if you arrived after a considerable amount of time, then you were free to camp as long as you were away by morning, in my opinion. Now that could be seen as rude, but I would be away by morning therefore I would not be able to gauge a reaction.

That night, the rain battered off the single-layered tent I had; it was not consistent. It was, however, a heavy downpour. It was enough to wake me up several times throughout the night, but I stayed strong and continued to rest.

That morning, I had my shower and hit the road, following the river Main. Again, I was in search of a place called Würzburg. I did not know why. All I knew was that it was helping me progress farther across the country and into the Czech Republic.

I came to a place called Miltenberg, a place I disliked right from the start, slap bang in the middle of nowhere. There was a supermarket there called DEKA, kind of like

Tesco but more advanced looking. I picked up my food for the day. The staff were a simple bunch of people. I felt like I had gone back in time, yet the store was very modern; the people were all over the age of forty and from the local villages, I assumed. I left to find that my bicycle had fallen over after I put it in one of the DEKA bicycle stands.

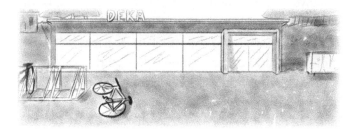

When home, I would write a stern letter of complaint to them regarding their poor-quality bicycle stands which buckled my front wheel and their poor service, if I would be feeling up to it. As I was cycling, I was unsure if it was the front wheel keeping me back or the wind. I came to the conclusion that it was most likely the wind, but the bicycle had suffered an injury that was not fatal.

I arrived at a place called Freudenburg, a small village. I followed the signs to get out of the place, and as I was doing so, I must have come off the cycle path as I was in the middle of nowhere but close to the river Main. I noticed a lake from the path and headed past a reception-like building and a bit farther. There was an elderly couple who had a problem with the brakes on their bicycle. I took a look at it and realised that I would need tools; therefore, I was not able to help them.

The lake was surrounded by well-maintained grass, and at one of the corners, there were diving boards. I cycled around to the corner closest to the boards, hopped off the bicycle, and changed into a different pair of shorts. The diving boards were springboards, but I was not entirely sure if it would be completely safe. How was I to know if the water was at the correct level? There was no one present on this oddly shaped day.

I used the diving board, which was a metre off the ground, and did a wee dive and enjoyed myself for a brief period, but I was too afraid to go off the three-metre board as I was unsure if the water was even deep enough, and I did not want to be scraping my nose off a rock underwater or even a trolley for that matter. Although this place was well out of way, I doubted there would have been a trolley. Maybe this was just my experience of the other rivers when the water level was low, but this was a man-made lake. The area looked abandoned apart from the well-maintained grass. Then again, it could be the wild animals who looked after it.

I packed up and got back on the saddle. Risking injury was not for me. I didn't want to render myself non-operational at the beginning of my travels.

I asked for directions, which pointed back to Freudenburg. I backtracked again. I headed forwards a few kilometres. I crossed a bridge and was back on the road. Again, the wind was right in front, making it harder than usual to cycle. These harsh elements were keeping me from progressing at my desired speed; it was only natural.

As I progressed farther down the road, I came across a barley field with patches of grass where one could have picnics or if there were people, a social event. As I was cycling, I began to belt out 'Danny Boy', which reminded me of home, and I had to take a few minutes' rest to catch a breath and get a grip. Basically, this was depressing.

I was on the road to Würzburg. The road signs had said it was another forty kilometres. *Great, not too far away*, I thought. Eventually, the road came to a motorway; and well, bicycles are not allowed on the motorway. I didn't know why, and I didn't want to find out. I would leave that for another time.

I headed back to the river Main and for a place called Marktheidenfeld. I arrived and asked a local couple if they knew how to get to Würzburg. They advised that I should stick to the river Main as it was so picturesque and scenic. For several days, that was all I had looked at. I needed a change.

I found a cycle post pointing to Karlstadt. It was a choice of sixty kilometres versus twenty kilometres. I took the risk and headed uphill. As I said before, any journey that started uphill was not one for me. This time, I went for it. The German countryside was picturesque. There were many barley fields and coniferous and evergreen trees that made up the forest and plenty of wildlife. I saw several yellow-coloured deer loitering about the roads and fields. I also saw plenty of watchtowers along the side of the roads.

This got me thinking, *Am I going to be shot at tonight?* No. It was either a training camp or for the hunters. I concluded it was for the hunters as there were plenty of deer to be shot that kept on crossing the road. I kept going; the sun was setting. It was a hot pinkish yellow colour burning in the sky; it was something else. I was going to take a picture, but that sunset was just for me; plus, I probably had no charge in a camera.

At one stage, I thought I was going to be hunted considering I was in hillbilly land with no villages around—you know, traveller on a bicycle, two backpacks, easily disposed of in one of the forests, not a trace, no whereabouts. Luckily, that did not happen. Oh Germany, what a country.

I came across a small reclused church and graveyard surrounded by forest, right in the middle of nowhere where I had been cycling. I had some dinner and paid my respects to the dead, thinking deeply and reflecting. I spent about ten minutes here before departing. Once the food had set in my stomach, I left.

I continued cycling and came across a forest; at the end, there was a sign for Karlstadt, only five kilometres away. *I will do that in the morning. Nice to know.* I set up camp and had a fire to charge my phone a little and then headed to bed. Two times that night, I had to relocate my tent because of the ground. I thought the foliage beneath the tent would act as a mattress. How wrong I was. Later on, it just turned out to be sore.

As I was sleeping, I could hear trains coming and going all night long. I had a sip of water to help soothe me. This did not really help, but at the same time, the trains were not really giving me too much bother. Reflecting on this instance, it bothered me a little as in this rather tranquil forest, there were trains passing. I was about several hundred metres from the track, and it was too late to relocate the tent to any real distance to avoid the sound. The reason I had chosen this location was for security and safety from any falling branches and from people. The bicycle was locked up around a tree.

In the end, it was too noisy for my liking, although there were no real barriers put in place to rebound the noise, only the wildlife. When I left the forest, I came across the largest solar farm I had ever seen, though I had not seen many. It spread across acres, thousands of photovoltaic plates in full view of the sun, green energy. I slept the night well regardless.

I got myself to Karlstadt and quickly headed for Würzburg. There was not much there, some statues, not that magnificent. I powered on through, and that night, I got myself to Kitzingen, a nice place on the riverfront. I arrived, locked up my bicycle, and headed to the river Main. I met a person there, and we had a joke and a laugh. Then a few of their friends came over, and we shared a few flasks of water. We sat around for about an hour or two before parting ways.

When I was with them, one decided to go for a swim in the river. It looked calm enough. I would have swam to the other side, but I was not risking it. A quick dip was enough. The first person I was with asked if I wanted to go for pizza. I declined the offer as I really didn't want this pizza. I headed for a place called Weissenfeld, and that was the last I saw of them.

The cycle towards Weissenfeld was some cycle through the countryside, flat plains through many fields, a lot of barley or grain being cut.

The sky was clear, and the stars were out; also, there was plenty of wildlife. I stopped and asked someone if they knew where I could find a campsite; apparently, one was not far away. I looked at the map and cycled towards it. This road had an incline of about ten degrees. I powered on, but there was no sign of camping, plenty of fields though. I came across a theme park outside a place called Geiselwind, with plenty of free parking spaces to place the tent for the night on the grass. I decided to call it a night as it was nearly midnight, and I had found a decent place to camp for the night. Grass was great to camp on, almost a luxury, which reminded me of having a wee snooze in Dubai, United Arab Emirates.

It was the middle of the afternoon. I was snoozing on the grass, and then all of a sudden, it started raining in an oscillating manner; all I felt was water coming down, and I jumped up as soon as I could. It was the irrigation system. That grass was great. There was a slim chance of camping there at that spot but not impossible in Dubai. I camped for more than twenty days in one of the most expensive cities in the world according to the masses—not this traveller. Anyway, that would be part two. I would get there, but for now, I experienced the monotonicity of Europe.

In the morning, the sun was shining through the tent; it was warmer than usual. It must have been about ten o'clock. I got ready and headed to the theme park, leaving the tent in the parking space. The theme park was twenty-two euros for a day. I decided against this park as, from the looks of things, I had been to better ones.

I was in the middle of nowhere once again, surrounded by fields and wildlife. I came across a bicycle sign for Ebrach and went for it. A few hours later of cycling in the heat, I arrived at a place called Bamberg. I did not like this place. I decided to use a locker at the tourist office to store my belongings for the afternoon while I had lunch, which was very handy. I enjoyed the lunch but not Bamberg. To me, if you really wanted to enjoy Bamberg, you would be expected to spend money. As a traveller, I didn't have time for that. It was mostly in the sun as it was shining high in the summer. To have a nice shaded area under an umbrella, you were expected to buy a meal or a drink or two to ensure the pleasantness, which was normal, but you shouldn't have to spend money to have pleasantness. Why should one have to spend money to have an enjoyable time? One should be content with themselves.

If I was with someone, it may have been a more enjoyable experience, but I doubted it. To whoever is reading this, I would advise you to go to Bamberg. If Bamberg was an inanimate object, it would be a bundle of sticks.

That evening, I was slow to move. It could have been the diet throughout the day or the fact that Bamberg had drained the life out of me. One point of interest was that, in Bamberg, there was a large bridge crossing the river

Regnitz, and there were people jumping off the bridge into the water. This attracted my attention, but I was not going to risk it. I would know for the next time if I ever happened to pass in, say, an automobile or maybe even on a bicycle. I just don't know; it did have its charm, just not for me. That bridge would be the only attraction for myself.

When I did hop back on the saddle, I aimed for a place called Waischenfeld. That night on the way, I came across a campsite. By the time I got there, the reception was closed. I waited until someone, possibly an employee or caretaker, came over. We chatted. They spoke in German. I spoke predominantly in english with German. All I wanted to do was sleep. The person asked for three euros in the end. I put my hand in my pocket and pulled out one euro and fifteen cents. They pointed to the corner of the *platz* and put up seven fingers, meaning seven o'clock in the morning. I slept, and did not even have time for a shower that morning. And I had lost track of the cycle way.

I continued on the path from the night before, which took me to a dual carriageway. At the time, I didn't feel like doing that cycle, although there was a path parallel for cyclists. I gave that a go and then gave up and headed back past the *campingplatz* in search of signs for Waischenfeld or at least the closest village. This was where a mobile phone with connectivity would be a very helpful tool; it would have told me exactly where to go, which would take out the pressure of the unknown. I embraced the unknown, but it can be tedious when you don't have the common technology.

It was a long cycle in the heat that I had not expected to do, and I wasn't feeling the freshest. I arrived, and the first thing I did was find a nice area in the shade to have my lunch. Later on, I discovered it was a government building.

I cycled around the small municipality. There was not much there—some shops, hotels, and a high street. I eventually had enough and headed for Kulmbach. This was mid-afternoon, so it was a pleasant cycle, though water was needed.

Along the way, I came across a sign for Hollfeld. I checked the map, and it was closer to the Czech Republic, and I followed. At one stage, I questioned the route, had a seat at the side of the road, and contemplated. Did I want to go through the process of continually cycling up and down hills with luggage? I pondered and eventually continued in the direction of Hollfeld, up and down through the German hills. At one point, I knew there was no going back, similar to Würzburg except I was able to backtrack that as I had not travelled too far; but in reality, it felt like much more.

I continued on through. Reflecting, I should have stayed on the original path I had chosen. At the time, I thought this route would be easier, not that I was wrong. I did have a very enjoyable cycling experience, though my energy levels were decreasing. Time for a refuelling, or maybe I needed water.

I arrived at Hollfeld, a small village twenty kilometres from nowhere. I stopped on a bench on the main road and had something to eat, a recharge. A person walked past. 'Hallo', said the person. They spoke in German. We spoke. I pulled out the map, and I asked about the terrain and the surroundings. They created a wave with their hand, suggesting that there would be patches of flats and hills. *Good information*, I thought. They pointed me out the way to go, and I headed that way. Paper maps were only good for the main roads, especially when you were using road maps. They took you a direct route.

Along the way, there was a Jesus monument right in the middle of nowhere. *Does something happen to the people who travel through this way? Is there a murderer, and should I pray for my life? Is this a popular attraction, or am I one of the first to see this?* I sat there for a little while, I was bewildered. I continued having something to eat as it was rather peaceful, and the surroundings were powerful. Before departing into the unknown, I needed this. It was peaceful enough there, but it was quite random.

That night, I was in search of Bayreuth. There were several reasons I was heading there, closer to the border. I thought I had heard of it before. This was the largest city before the border. Beirut—now that was what I had heard of before.

The signs kept me right. I was getting closer. I was about ten kilometres away, and I came across a place called Eckersdorf, where there was a large crowd of people gathered together, another open-air event serving beer. It was basically a German market selling craft beer. Many tents with many pews—there was nothing really of interest here, only beer and Germans. I quickly made an exit, following a pointing green arrow which led me out of the place. I had spent enough time absorbing the German culture.

It was getting late, the sun had gone down, and the lights were turned on, on the bicycle. I powered on through to Bayreuth. I continued another kilometre before deciding to camp in a field. I knew that had I continued, I would have been within the city limits, and camping would have been much harder to find and usually illegal; well, I didn't want to have to pay a fine. Money could be better utilised and should be. When it came to a city, town, or municipality, it was best to camp before or after; or if you were hardcore in a safe and secure area free from people, basically, you don't want to be annoyed while you sleep. Be mindful of where you are.

I remember camping in Tehran, Iran. I was asked to leave the accommodation I had been staying at for being myself and I had to find alternative accommodation. I knew the area as I had been there a month or two. I remember camping in the city not far from the Indian consulate under a roof. It was secluded, however when morning arrived there were people about. I was even invited inside for a bite to eat and a cup of tea. Again, getting ahead of myself…

Wild camping was acceptable if you tidied up after yourself and were away at a reasonable time, gauged by the time of day or night. On weekdays, people may be up early to walk their dogs or head to work, whereas on weekends most people usually sleep longer; therefore, you can camp for longer periods to avoid the local council or police being informed by those local pests.

I had a fine sleep that night. When I awoke, the sun was shining. After a quick brushing of teeth in the sunlight in the middle of the field and getting a few bewildered looks from passers-by, I made tracks and headed for Bayreuth. I took a quick stop for food and then went into the town centre. I came across a market and picked up some fruit for the day ahead. I did not stay long. I had planned to enjoy my Friday night somewhere else other than Bayreuth.

I headed off in search of the border. I would have finished my lunch at around two o'clock in the afternoon before making tracks and hitting the road. This time, I pulled out my compass as I really did not have a notion of which direction I should be heading. I knew that this was not going to be easy as there was a lot of rural areas to be passed before I reached the border.

After deep breaths, I chose between cycle paths and main roads. Cycle paths were convenient, though when they stopped, they usually stopped. At least the road took you to your destination, be it carriageway or motorway. I was unsure which was more direct, but I can only assume that you eventually ended up where you wanted to be. The road I was on was the E49/48. I managed to hop onto this at Bayreuth, either that or heading through random villages. This road was more direct. And the paper road map of Europe basically guided me, I had no alternatives unless I came across a sign.

I cycled up and down nice-looking landscapes. Along the way through the German hills, you didn't know what to expect around each corner. I saw some nice rocks and trees, many trees and fields. I arrived at a place called Marktredwitz, which was only fifteen kilometres from the border. I just kept on going on the E48 as it was the most direct route.

There were many hills to climb before getting anywhere. This kept me back as, at times, I had to get off the bicycle and walk through it. The area had perfect walking conditions and scenery to absorb. I went for it, and I was going for it. There was about a kilometre left before the border.

I needed water. I called into a service station, but everything was closed. I went around the back and saw a group of people, possibly the owners. 'Kahn ich habe estow wasser, bitte?' I said.

'Yes, the tap is over there,' they replied. They then invited me to join them at their table and asked if I would like something to eat or drink. I passed on the food as I was asked if I were hungry. I was not, but I didn't pass on a drink. We drank jars of water for hours before I made the decision to hit the road again. Sound German people.

It was around eleven o'clock in the evening, and I could see the border in the distance. I got on my bicycle and pedalled slowly. This time, I was ready for the border, seeing as I could see it. How could I not make it? A kilometre had passed, and I had broken into the Czech Republic.

CZECH REPUBLIC

This morning, I was aiming for Cheb. It was too far to complete the journey the previous evening as I was wrecked from the cycling that day; plus, it was dark at night-time which could prove to be dangerous. It seemed fairly safe to be camping past the border.

I came across a service station on the border which had a truck stop. I set up camp at the side of the station and slept the night away. The noise from the station did not affect the sleep nor did the passing vehicles on the dual carriageway.

When I finally arose from my slumber, I was feeling fresh. After some food and the washing of my face, I was golden. I headed for Cheb along what I believed to be a dual carriageway. Many drivers beeped their horns as I was cruising along the road. I took no notice really; more didn't beep than beeped, so it wasn't too noticeable, but I noticed. Still, I waved to them all.

I cycled about ten kilometres before I reached Cheb. I saw a sign for a Tesco and headed towards it as I wanted some known food, but Lidl got the better of me. I went to pay, and I asked if I can pay in euro, but it was not accepted here. I had thought that European countries used euro and only euro, hence the title. In the shop, they had expected me to pay in the Czech koruna. Then I remembered that in the North of Ireland, they use pound sterling; and in the south, they use euro. It was a mad world, not that I remembered, but in other European countries, the currency was usually euro. Food was not purchased here. Luckily, I had some supplies, and I was able to pick up more at the local garage for those extra calories.

Before setting off for Karlovy Vary, I had to brace myself for what I was about to do—fifty kilometres of dual carriageway or maybe motorway continuously, no stops, pedal to the metal. I entered the road, and I saw a picture of a car on a road sign. No bicycles were seen.

I was already on the road. I was just going to pretend that I did not see that sign—best to be ignorant. But if I were pulled over by the police or other authority, I would have said that I had been on the road since Germany in the hope they would allow me to continue until I reached my destination. Anyway, I did a few spells on myself several times for my own general safety. As I was cycling, it was rather dangerous. Though the only problem with cycling on the road was that when it came to a junction, you would have to wait for the flowing traffic to pass before crossing; and of course, you would be using the Highway Code to be on the safe side. Many times, I had thought about coming off at each junction, but I powered on like a trooper as it was the most direct route to the unknown place of Karlovy Vary. I knew what I was getting myself into, I was prepared to take the risk, and I knew it was not going to be easy.

About twenty kilometres before Karlovy Vary, there was a service station. I called in and refuelled the tank with nuts and raisins and then contemplated for a while. I managed to avoid an ambulance being escorted by the police. As I sat at the service station, an employee came out. They told me that you'd get a fine for cycling on the highways. My heart literally jumped a wee bit. They then told me that if I crossed the road, I can follow a river. I thought, *right, I have gotten this far. Might as well try an alternative route.*

I used a bridge to cross the highway; it was an overgrown, abandoned car park, no signs of a river. It was best to not investigate any further as that was really an unknown, like I would have been following a river in the hope that it would take me to where I wanted to go. This was where a mobile phone with connectivity would make things easy. In the distance of the service station, I could see fluorescent jackets and what appeared to be a police motorbike. It was best to chill and keep calm.

Time passed, and I gathered the courage to continue to my chosen destination along the original path I chose. Time passed, and the landscape was changing from forest to city. It took me by surprise. I was amazed. This was Czech Republic.

There was a sign for the centre farther down the road a few kilometres. I decided to get off the highway to catch my breath and not risk being caught in the city limits as I wondered what would happen to the bicycle if I were to be lifted by the authorities. I have now come to the conclusion that the road that I had been cycling on was, a motorway, hence the picture of the car at the start of the road but I am not certain. In my opinion, people who ride bicycles should be allowed on every road apart from the autobahn. It was the easiest way to cover distance. That cycle was daunting.

I took the exit before the centre and was on the outskirts of the city. *No problem*, I thought. I had been on the road long enough. When I was there, it began to rain. I took shelter under the highway I had just devoured. From there, I found the path to the city centre. Along the way, I found a McDonald's, bought a cheeseburger, and used the Wi-Fi. Oh, wait, there was none. They must be cutting back on their costs at McDonald's in Karlovy Vary; maybe it was not needed here.

I headed into the centre of Karlovy Vary, which was a lovely city to look at. The architecture was nice—high-rise buildings in a Victorian fashion or, as I read, Renaissance; many buildings which protruded from the valleys; and a forest which lept out from behind the buildings. First time here, and I would go back. It was quite a spectacular city. Old town and new town were separate. Old was nice to walk about; everything looked pristine. There was definitely a street and a fountain in one of them. It was old-fashioned funnily enough and looked a little grimy though polished.

I found a restaurant off the high street and refuelled in a watering hole. I drank jars of water and rested until I found somewhere to stay for the evening. Before this, I went to one of the many cash exchange vendors to change banknotes over. The majority of the banknotes that I had had been from the Bank of Scotland and were not accepted. They were only accepting english pound sterling, which I found frustrating. What sort of united kingdom was this? I assumed this was because of the upcoming independence referendum in Scotland which would be in September. It was only the start of August. I was nearly enraged as the money I had worked hard for was not welcomed to be changed into the currency that I needed. *Oh well*, I thought, *I have enough koruna to do me the day or two that I am here.*

I went to another restaurant to have lunch and, in doing so, got talking to a person who spoke english and was able to tell me there were no hostels in Karlovy Vary. *Great*, I thought. *I will have to find alternative accommodation.* We parted ways and had arranged to meet later on; they were Czech, nice person.

I set off looking for a place to camp for the evening. I went back to the river to see if there was somewhere safe to camp. As I was cycling, I came across people with camping gear, or maybe it was just yoga mats. I can't remember. Anyway, I stopped and asked them if they knew of a campsite. They did not. An average Czech walked past, and I asked if they knew where I could place a tent for the night or at least somewhere to sleep. They had shopping bags on them and asked me to wait for five minutes.

I complied as they must have had something for me. They did not speak a word of english.

We walked, they made a few stops, and I waited. Eventually, we got to somewhere that looked very dodgy, almost like the 'InShops' in Belfast city centre. I did not know what was happening. The whole language barrier was something else, but I persisted. I wasn't sure if I was going to get robbed or stabbed. I felt safe regardless. The worse thing to happen would probably be to get stabbed and then robbed. I did not know what was happening or when it was going to happen.

Eventually, I was given a key and shown to a room—single bed, sofa, and a cupboard. For six pound sterling, it was not too bad. This place was top-notch after camping for seven nights or so; this was what I needed, a bed in a secure room. At this stage, the main person who helped me had left. I was left with a Czech called Marrion. Now they did all the talking for me when securing a room, so it was right to give them some koruna to help them out. How they showed me they needed money was to repeatedly go, 'baby need nom nom.' And they pretended to spoon-feed themselves. I knew what they were playing at and complied with them as they had helped me secure a room. Otherwise, it would have been camping in the wet. Whether or not the money I gave Marrion all went for 'nom nom' was another story.

Time passed, and they handed me a slip of paper saying 'Kona 200Kr.' Did Marrion just hand me a receipt? I didn't know what they were hinting at, at the time. But they were telling me that they wanted two hundred koruna for advising me to put my bicycle in my room. I was flabbergasted and was kind of like, *I would have been doing that anyway. That bicycle is like my home. Without it, it would be very hard to be doing what I am doing and what I am going to do, though it could be replaced.*

What happened with Marrion only highlighted the problems people faced every day when they don't have the money they need to support their families. When walking the streets at night, there were many strange characters who were flying about the place, from one side of the street to the other. It would appear that instead of dealing with their problems head on, they preyed on the newest members of their community, as well as drinking iced water, which was very common in the Middle East and Asia.

It was getting late, and I decided to call it a night and headed back to my room to have a little overpriced water. The person I was supposed to meet earlier—well, I had other things on my mind. *Where is the fresh water at? The clean European water they speak of, where is it?*

On Monday, I was awoken by the sound of builders outside working on a dilapidated old building. They were refurbishing the building. Fair enough.

The first task on the agenda that morning was to get more money changed. I went to several banks, about ten different exchange shops, and five hotels who all did not accept Scottish pound sterling. This put me into a downward spiral. How would I eat? How would I survive without money? I was not ready for this yet. Only when I have no money would my game plan change from frivolous to hunter to survivalist. For now, I would continue to live like a traveller with the remaining money because everything was going to be all right, and I got to not worry about a thing.

It was a nice dark night in the Czech Republic, with the street lights creating an ambient effect which made the town look even more special. The lights were flickering off the buildings, and the trees were blowing in the wind; it really was special on the autumnal night. I assumed, for the people who lived there, it was normal. But as a foreigner, I enjoyed the lights and the architecture.

I came across a hotel that I had not been into yet, and I went in to see about getting money changed—success. The reason for the success was that there was a younger clerk on the cashier's desk, and I assumed they would be less informed about the pound sterling; therefore, changing the Scottish pound sterling was not a problem. I now had more money to spend in this wonderful place or to get me through the Czech Republic. I was happier. On the way back to the hostel, I stopped at a restaurant for a feed and jars of water. It was good food for a bad day, but in the end, everything worked out.

I returned to the hostel which was probably the lowest-grade accommodation that I had ever stayed in. In Czech Republic, they are called *ubytovna*, which means 'hostel'.

I also thought this can be permanent accommodation for those who did not have a home, kind of like a hostel but cheap for a foreigner. I planned to leave Karlovy Vary in search of Prague in the morning.

That night at the hostel, it was very loud in the rooms parallel, but I did not let this bother me in my quest for sleep. Most people definitely would have complained or done something to enhance their surroundings, but I slept through it. There was actually no chance to complain anyway. I stayed put and continued to read as I found interest in a book I found on a bookshelf. It was called *The Knowledge of Power*. All I wanted to know was where it was heading.

That morning, I read another few chapters and then decided it was time to get up in search of a way out of Karlovy Vary. I had to find an Internet station. I came across a computer in one of the shopping centres. This would be the second shopping centre I had entered on these travels; that was not a great deal to me. I needed to use the Internet to find a way out of Karlovy Vary and to communicate back home and afar.

After using the PC with the Czech keyboard, which was similar but not identical to an english keyboard, it was time to have bad food. I saw a McDonald's, and they were doing two large Big Mac meals for two hundred koruna, which was about six pound sterling. From there, I proceeded down to a grassy courtyard with plenty of trees equally spaced to write in the book to release what was on my mind.

All I can say was I thought the Czechs were a little light-headed—well, not all of them. But this was what I experienced in Karlovy Vary. Here, I noticed a dramatic change in the type of person. Or maybe I was that exhausted and needed to find a safe place to sleep for the night that I asked and trusted the first person who was available to help. And they did a great job. Or maybe I was in the rough side of town with the cheap prices. Either way, I did have a great time in this little city; it was a change from the norm. Maybe I would have had a different experience had I asked another person. Then again, I should have, would have, could have but did not.

I began my cycling down the river Ohře, my bicycle and I. It was actually quite a depressing ride as the weather was not great, and I had not the best experience of Karlovy Vary because of money issues. Other than that, I would ask you all to visit Karlovy Vary if you were in Czech Republic, some place and some friendly people.

I cycled down the river some fifty kilometres. Now this was like no other river cycling I had done, not that it was dangerous, but having luggage on the back of me, I could not fully enjoy it. I did enjoy it; I just knew that it would have been better if I had less. Cycling the rivers in Germany was paved tarmac and almost flat. Over in Czech, you were following almost untouched cycling trails. But in my honest opinion, this was what I had wanted.

I kept on cycling until it got too dark to cycle anymore and decided to camp for the night. I decided to place my tent just before a forest as it was completely dark and well I had no idea what to expect late at night. In the morning, I could hear one or two cars passing as I had placed my tent close but not on a driveway. It was a small patch of grass next to the river Ohře. Anyway, I placed my tent under a huge sycamore, which helped protect me from the rain which was pouring down overnight. I decided it was time to get up.

The amount of slugs that had crawled up my tent and slept there was remarkable, and there was one wee hallion who snuck into the tent. It was time to shake and disassemble. Goodbye, slugs. Hello, forest.

That morning, I headed for a place called Klášterec. That was where I had planned to camp the previous night but decided not to go any farther because of the weather and the time. I arrived, quickly used the bathroom, and went into the tourist office to get some information. The person behind the counter was extremely handsome. That was all the information that was gathered. They were helpful enough, and we had a laugh.

A truck driver then helped me and gave me directions. They asked if I wanted to go the long or short way. I answered short. They gave me some directions, and I followed. After crossing a bridge a few kilometres into the journey, I was thinking, *Surely, this is the wrong way. I am going towards Karlovy Vary but on the opposite side of the river.* I continued a short while before returning the way I had come. I was trusting the instructions given to see if they were right.

I stopped outside a house, someone came over, and I asked them what direction it was to Prague. They didn't speak english but were able to find a family member who could help with the language barrier. They told me to go the other way and a few other directions. Back I went. I thought I had travelled some distance, but in reality, it was only a few kilometres, ten at maximum.

I continued through the countryside, up and down the hills; it was rather enjoyable following the Czech cycle ways, which would need a map as they were only a number, with the occasional city listed. I was exhausted. I came across a place called Kadaň, which was a fairly picturesque municipality, and decided it was time for lunch.

I saw a sign for a place called Žatec. The person I had asked mentioned to travel there and ask for more information from the tourist office. I proceeded to Žatec and then to a place called Louny. There, I had my tea outside a car wash.

It was empty, but there was a picnic table. I was able to have my tea and check the map for direction. The car wash attendant came out, and I introduced myself and said that I was going to Prague. I pulled out the map once again, and at this point, I saw a sign for Prague—handy.

Previously when cycling through the countryside in the middle of nowhere, there was a random Czech with a bottle of beer in one hand and a stick in the other who was talking to themselves. I assumed they were a farmer. It was funny to see on such a depressing day due to the weather, and morale was not as high until I got back on the road.

I was able to cycle up the dual carriageway about forty kilometres to a place called Slaný, where I camped for the night. However, that was not true. I had several jars of water beforehand in the centre, and I was camping in Slaný, right in the middle or close to the city limits at the side of the road in a grassy area with trees and that.

A couple walked past and had a wee snigger, and about ten minutes later, the police happened to be sitting across the road. At this stage, I was not in the tent. I was fiddling with the bicycle. They came over and asked me what I was up to. 'You cannot camp here,' they told me.

'I am heading for Prague in the morning, and there is a sign right there,' I replied.

'I am sorry, we can escort you to a hotel,' they replied.

'No thank you,' I replied.

'Okay, follow us, and we will take you to a campsite,' they replied. They then escorted me to the town boundary and told me to cycle two kilometres and that I would find a campsite.

I cycled about a kilometre, found a field, and placed camp to be up early in the morning. I awoke to the sound of cars passing. It was my time to go. I had several handfuls of plums growing from the trees close to my tent before leaving in search of Prague. I decided to head into the centre as the sign that had caught my eye the night before was for the motorway, and I did not want to risk any more police trouble for cycling somewhere I know I cannot be. I got to the centre, picked up supplies for the day, checked the maps, and headed for the place called Kladno.

Now it was not an easy trip to get to Prague on a bicycle from twenty kilometres away. It was mostly accessible via motorway. I continued to cycle through small villages in the hope I would reach Prague eventually. I could see airplanes taking off in the distance, and I knew I was getting closer. After some more windy country roads, I could sense I was getting closer, but where to go? I was on the outskirts of the city, and I had to cycle several kilometres around the airport again as it was mainly accessible via motorway.

Eventually, I came to a small village, refuelled once more, and decided to buy a large bottle of Coca-Cola to keep the energy levels maintained. I then found a person on the road and asked for directions as I had no idea where I was going. 'That way', they said.

'Sound', I replied.

About a kilometre later, I saw a sign for the centre, though there was no distance mentioned. All I wanted to do was get to the centre. I thought I was in the centre as it had looked fairly busy, with various watering holes scattered throughout the area as well as much passing traffic. I found myself a hostel for three hundred and fifteen koruna. I decided to have a wander and see what other accommodation was available. I returned.

'Two nights, please', I said to the attendant. Money was exchanged with the attendant. Time to get into a room with four walls and relax in Prague.

That night, I decided not to venture too far into the town as I had planned to stay here for a few nights, not that I had planned, but I needed rest for a few days in a place with nice surroundings. I wanted to leave everything else for the Friday and the weekend. That night, I had my rest and was awoken to the sound of buses in the morning. This was not what I had hoped for; at least when you camped in the wild, you were surrounded by nature—most of the time.

In the morning, I found a place for breakfast and ate. When I asked someone for directions to the centre, they advised that I take the tram or bus. 'No thank you, I have a bicycle,' I said.

I was staying in Praha six, which was a few kilometres from the Prague Castle, which I used as a landmark. This was my first experience of the city—a large castle, cathedral, building, and structure.

Actually, the first stop was in a garden to eat lunch. It was a good-looking garden. I enjoyed my lunch in front of a statue and walked around the grounds. I then proceeded into the castle in search of something. When I had finished my castle walk, I headed into the centre. There was nothing eventful there, plenty of tourists and people of different ethnicities trying to sell you a wide variety of goods.

It was nearly teatime, so I decided to head back to the hostel via the Charles Bridge.

What a nice bridge with many different statues which all told a story. I headed up some steps to get back to the castle; by the time I got to the top of the steps, sweat was pouring off me. It was the opposite of baltic.

That night, I had a shower and some food and headed off into the Prague centre in search of something, maybe something I had not done before. The night was early. I should have listened to the hostel reception worker who advised me to go to a club in 'Praha 7'. But as usual, I didn't take the advice into real consideration. They told me to go via tram, but I had the bicycle with me, and yes, I could have locked it up, but I was thinking about how I would return home later that evening; that'd cost extra travel money that could be spent on food and water. This was the start of my travel session. I wanted to try to extend the money; plus, it sounded like too much effort. And you know the score, no connected device to whip up a map.

I headed off into the town on a Friday evening. There were far too many tourists for my liking, it was as if the city had been built for tourism. It was like a Western hive of mediocre music and tourist attractions. I was looking for something more on a Friday night. It was getting late.

I came across a seated area with people. I then sat down and decided to talk with two local people. They were a bit odd, but we had a laugh. I was travelling and having a sit-down, and there they were from the city sitting and admiring the Coal Market statue, not really that much, but I had a laugh with them and myself. I had a few jars of water that night. I had fun up until the point, where I decided to head in search of fast food.

As I sat in a restaurant, there were two young people next to me who were basically drooling over the food I had. I offered them some chips and half a burger, and we got chatting. One, who spoke very good english with an American twang, told me of a festival happening about thirty kilometres away from Prague that they were going to in the morning. We chilled for a while, and we headed off to a rock bar called Harley's for a drink. The place was a rip-off but catered to the locals and tourists. I had been given water out of a boot for free. After that, the english-speaking Czech said that they had to run a few errands and that they would be back. I did not know who to trust in the Czech Republic.

I decided to call it a night, picked up my bicycle, and headed for the hostel. I took my usual route through the castle; at the time I was there, the grounds were closed for the night, so I had to find an alternative way around. I ended up taking a wrong turn and must have been cycling well into the morning. The cobbled streets destroyed the panniers that were attached to carry a secondary backpack. The vibrations from the movement over the cobbles caused the screws to become loose. I was exhausted and needed to find my bed.

Hours later, I came back to the castle and headed a different direction, eventually ending up at the hostel.

Even one of the guards told me I couldn't go through; I was raging. I thought they had a sword. Best to leave it at that.

That morning, I was awoken to the sound of someone trying to batter the door down as it was time to check out.

This was not what I wanted to hear after several hours of sleep. That person sounded like a wild beast. Angry and annoyed they were. It was a student hostel after all; what else would they be expecting? I had a lived experience. Or maybe it was different in Prague. They must be eager to learn.

I checked out, left my backpacks in the storage facility, and decided to pick up supplies for breakfast and lunch. I found a park and had my lunch. I saw several homeless people, made them some food, and gave it to them; they were very grateful. Most people are happy when they receive food, homeless or not. It was the gesture that counted. I spent some time with them and then made tracks. Prague did have a few homeless people through the various areas of the city. They were not so much on the streets begging but loitering about, usually more than one too.

This made me think, which should make you think. Homeless people are not all on the streets for the same reasons or circumstances. There are many reasons, I supported them regardless. But not all people are homeless because of what we think. Next time you see a homeless person, appreciate their struggle.

I headed back to the hostel to see about another bed for the night. They advised of another student hostel a few blocks away which had the same price. That night, I found my bed and slept there until Sunday morning.

That morning, I went out in search of a famous building I had seen in a movie, possibly an action movie from the millennium. I found several, many asking for an admission fee, which I found ridiculous. What would happen if somebody actually wanted to go there for spiritual meaning?

That night, I went to the previous hostel and paid for another bed, this time on the south side of the building, where there were no buses present. I had a good enough sleep. Pity the checkout was at ten o'clock in the morning, but I was up on time.

That Monday, I ventured around the town for a second time. It was a lovely city to look at. I even headed up to one of the highest points to get one of the best panoramic views of the city. Monday night, I was meeting someone for dinner. An average cheeseburger and chips. I think it was to provide information on my current whereabouts, health, and general well-being. Fair enough. I was happy to enjoy a meal.

That night, I headed back to the hostel. It was getting late, and I did not want to pay for another room as I was going to be there until early morning before I left in search of a way out of the Czech Republic. I had asked if I could stay in the luggage room. 'No', replied the attendant.

How boring! I had been sitting on some rather comfortable chairs in the foyer of the hostel, but I could not sleep there as I need to be straight when I sleep or at least comfortable in a horizontal position. Eventually, I was given a room. I was not allowed to sleep on the bed, which was understandable. A few hours passed, and I crept into the bed for a few good hours of sleep before heading off down the river Vltava.

That morning, I awoke to the pleasant sound of a knock on the door asking me to pack up my belongings and to vacate the room. I complied. Out the door I go and on my bicycle. I took one more look at Prague from the bicycle as I left. It was a real city—unclean streets, cobwebs on the statues, and many homeless people about the streets; nothing was hidden. Welcome to the Czech Republic. Off I headed down the river to more unknown territory.

I cycled about twenty kilometres before getting the map out to see where I was as I had split off the river Vltava. I passed many campsites along the way, and how I wanted to sleep, but it was much too early, and all I wanted to do was get back on the road. I powered on, eventually coming to a dead end, only to ask a local how to get back to the river. I asked them what path I should take to get back to the river. They pointed to the train tracks which crossed over the river, which I was once following.

I hopped off my bicycle, took a deep breath, and proceeded to cross. All I could think about was that film *Stand by Me* and what were to happen if a train came. Anyway, I crossed the bridge and was back to the main road—handy. Time to cover some distance.

A few days had passed, and I arrived in a place called České Budějovice, a small town with a nice square where one could eat their lunch as I did. I was able to find out more information other than the name. From the tourist office, I was given a variety of cycle maps which included all the numbers of the cycle ways and a map of the country, very handy. Pity I never received this upon entering the country. I was offered them in Karlovy Vary, but you had to pay for them, and well, I would rather not have had them. I should have asked for the manager. I made it this far with a map of Germany. Before this, I was cycling through some delicious-looking landscapes through the Czech hills. From road to field, I was equipped. About the maps, yes, there were some yellow signs with a number on them and others with the name of the municipality. Had I had the maps, it would have been much easier to navigate. It was a mixture of yellow signs and road signs, but the yellow ones had various numbers that corresponded to the map. At times, I was taken through fields and lakes, definitely not for everyone on a bicycle. Well, that would depend on the type of bicycle chosen.

I was able to direct myself to another smaller place called Český Krumlov, where I spent about an hour eating lunch and having a look at the large rocks as well as watching the massive number of kayaks going down the river. It was rather peaceful and tranquil as there was only the odd car passing on the road and minimal noise from the kayaks. Plus, the tree branches were hanging over the road, creating an arch-like effect—pure greatness.

That would have been fun to do. *Another time*, I thought.

From here, I was able to get myself back on the road which followed the river Vltava to near the border of Austria. Good cycling was had on this road. There was plenty of nature.

I reached an area of the river which had a sign for the place of Linz in Austria; it sounded like a funny place—a place I was in several years ago but not physically. Austria was the country I was aiming for. I had my last meal and final jar of Czech water in an authentic Czech restaurant. I had a Hawaiian pizza and used the Wi-Fi to map exactly where I was. Half an hour had passed, and I was past the border of Austria.

AUSTRIA

Now these hills were really alive with the sound of music. There were many hills and many small villages in the rural areas. I was on a main road which consisted of plenty of hills, which equalled downward momentum to push me up the next hill, which was great; once I cycled to the top of the hill, it was easy riding.

About two or three hours had passed, and I was in the city of Linz. I called into a garage to ask for directions to a campsite. There was one not far away from a lake. I cycled a fair bit before asking a couple if they knew where I could find a campsite. They were very helpful, and I was very polite. They showed me where to go as they were heading to the lake also.

I arrived to the lake. I went for a swim to cool down after the day of cycling. I had lunch and then went to the campsite. The campsite was full of families. I asked a restaurant owner if I could place a tent for the night—success. The tent was assembled, and it was time to see what Linz had to offer on a Friday night.

When I headed off into the centre, it was beginning to get darker, and the city was lit up. Across the river Danube, you could see the reflection of the buildings on the other side; it was a fairly beautiful sight. Plus, the large number of LED lights helped create an ambient and modern feel to the city.

I parked up my bicycle in the centre and had a walk around, eventually bumping into a group of local Austrians who could speak english well enough that I could chat with them and have a bit of craic. They were young though—well, younger than I was. Everyone on the street on a Friday night was young, or maybe I had gotten older. Sixteen to eighteen was the average age, or maybe the people look younger over there, something about their Austrian genes maybe.

The night progressed, and it was beginning to get late. I bumped into a person who was heading in the same direction down the river Danube. They showed me to a party happening on a still boat on the riverfront. *Okay,* I thought. I went in and enjoyed myself for an hour and then headed back to the campsite. The night was nearly over; all that was on the menu was jars of water. It was a great start to a Saturday morning.

I headed back to the tent, locked up the bicycle, and slept. I was up early that day. I had some breakfast. While cleaning the tent, I accidentally snapped one of the flimsy tent poles of the set. I would fix that at a later date. I spoke to another camper who was also travelling with a bicycle. They were also cycling, though they had planned exactly where they were going and how long it would take them, they had an itinerary. They were heading for Budapest. I got out the map and had a look.

'All right, do you mind if I follow for a bit? If I can keep up, that is,' I said to the person.

We both packed up our gear, split the scene, and began cycling. We headed for Krems, about one hundred kilometres from Linz. Before we left, they even got my CatEye speedometer working. They were able to align the device with the sensor that would be able to track my speed and distance as I travelled. For over a month, I had been travelling with this device, and it was inactive until this cyclist showed me how to set it up. Yes, they were a cyclist; I was not. They even told me the clothing I was wearing was not aerodynamic enough to be cycling due to the air resistance caused by the cloth flapping about; they even had a wee snigger, which made me laugh as well. I was here for fun, not to be aerodynamic.

Kilometres passed, and I decided it'd be best to pick up supplies for the long road ahead. We stopped at a Eurospar. I took longer than expected to do my shop, not that I was on a budget as such; the shop was overpriced compared with every other supermarket I have visited. It was as if they were only in places where you were desperate, and there were no alternatives.

When I went outside, they were gone. Oh, the horror. But I only would have kept them back in the long run, and we had agreed if I could not keep up, we would split. Common courtesy would have been nice though. They were French Mexican. I wasn't quite sure.

They had gotten me on a path that, with many kilometres of cycling, would get me to Vienna and then to Budapest—the Donauradweg, which follows the river Danube. This path was the easiest to cycle, although after about one hundred kilometres after Linz, the wind really got to me, and my speed would have dropped to less than fifteen or ten kilometres per hour. It was a tough cycle after the sun had dropped and the temperature. 'If only I had tight Lycra clothing,' I jested. This path was a mixture of river, road, rural, and vineyards—great cycling—though road was best for distance. I arrived at Krems, found a campsite, and asked the price.

'Ten euros', the Austrian said.

'I will think about it,' I answered. This frustrated them. They began to get angry and informed their partner. I said I would ponder a little more.

'Nein danke. Auf Wiedersehen' I said with a grin on my face. Ten euros for ten hours of sleep? Not really worth it. No thank you. I got back to the river Danube and cycled another fifty kilometres before finding a place to camp on the riverfront until morning.

At half past eight in the morning, I was ready and back on the bicycle. It was less than one hundred kilometres to

Vienna, about seventy kilometres, easily done in a matter of hours. The sun was out, and at that time, there were many people on the Donauradweg.

From one side to the other, it was a continuous stretch. *I must be getting closer*, I thought. The sun was getting to me about thirty kilometres before Vienna. I had to hop into the river for a dip to cool down. I progressed onwards, eventually getting there, and the first stop was an Internet cafe to inform friends and family of my cycling accomplishment. I was ecstatic about what I had done in those two days. I was quite impressed with myself, the power of one.

After the Internet session, I went to a McDonald's to replenish the energy I had lost. Several cheeseburgers and a drink did it rightly. I zoomed through the town, found a hostel, had a shower, locked up my luggage for the afternoon, and ventured into the town with a young lawyer student who was visiting from Colombia. We started off in the museum quarter and then a fancy garden and then split ways as I wanted to see what I could before leaving.

I arrived back to the hostel at around ten o'clock at night and used a computer to check emails. As I was going to check for a room, I decided against it as there was a sign saying 'No free rooms'. Fair enough. I got my belongings and went back on the bicycle at that time, and I picked up some supplies and headed off in search of the river Danube. Beforehand, I followed the city road signs to get me to the river, eventually coming to a garage where I bought a map for the same price of a room. The map of Austria was basically useless as I planned to leave the country by the next day, no returns on the map.

I found my way back to the river and proceeded on down about ten kilometres before placing the tent for the night—up early the next day and back on the Donauradweg, sort of. Apparently, I was on a little island and needed to cross over another bridge before getting back on the route. I asked an Austrian person who was happy to help. We cycled about ten kilometres before I was back on the road. 'Danke hew,' I said before leaving.

I was on the road again, another hot day of cycling. I was unsure of the temperature most of the time as I did not have a device for recording. And where can you find a thermometer on a river? Petrol stations sometimes have thermometers, but there were none in sight.

SLOVAKIA

Eventually, I hit the Slovakian border. Bratislava was to the left of me on the other side of the river. I didn't bother going over to have a look. I had been to a city before but not a Slovakian city to be fair. Next time, I will visit. From the other side of the river, it did look different. I continued on down the river in search of Hungary.

Throughout the day, there was a bit of cycling trouble. I met two Austrians who were on their way to Bratislava for coffee. They were lost as well. I can say and would say and may have said before that it was better to be lost with company than on your own, especially when on a bicycle and without connectivity to find out an exact route. Eventually, we got back on track, and I continued down the river Danube; they went for their coffee, I assumed.

At one stage, the Donauradweg just kind of ended. However, I did not have a map of the route, only a road map of Europe. So I continued, expecting to see a sign somewhere along the line. Eventually, I found a path for Gyor, Hungary. I proceeded.

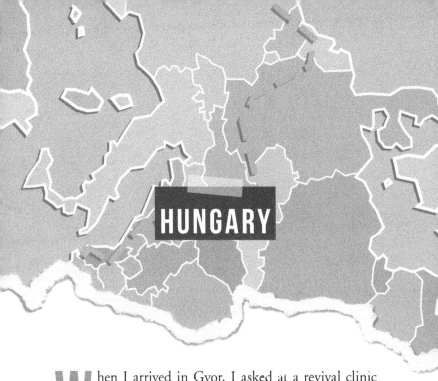

HUNGARY

When I arrived in Gyor, I asked at a revival clinic if I could place a tent until early morning. 'Yes', the person at the reception replied and told me to take a shower.

'In time, in time', I replied. I had my shower and slept that night.

The next morning, I packed up my gear and headed for Pápa and then Veszprem. I was road cycling again, very convenient. It would take you where you wanted to go, but during a lengthy cycle, you had to maintain speed and cannot get off the bicycle unless you found an area for rest.

As I got onto the number eighty-three road to Pápa, I came across someone who had broken down at the side of the road, a Hungarian person who had driven from england and had some more kilometres to complete before they would reach their destination. They began trying to sell me jackets, trainers, aftershave, basically the contents of the car.

I didn't need anything. They were a good person. At the same time, it was as if they were a random Hungarian at this car acting like it belonged to them, and they were trying to sell what they could out of it. This was just a perception; they were probably a genuine person. *Good person*, I thought regardless. They actually informed me of the Balaton Lake, which was in the centre of the country. I was able to give them some euros for their troubles as they were sound, and I had the change.

I proceeded seventy kilometres down the road. During my cycle, I received a large gash on the left calf from when I was stretching out on the bicycle and lost control; the metal pedal tore into my left calf muscle, leaving a large branding which became covered in oil and hair. I didn't let this faze me and continued cycling, eventually coming to what looked like roadworks. I decided to get off the road for some lunch before getting back on the saddle. Sometimes I'd think, *What if?* I'd run many scenarios through the head that much could go wrong. But it was only a thought. I knew it can be dangerous at times, and it'd be best to remain calm and relaxed but focussed.

I was back on the road, cool, calm, and collected. I was the only bicycle on the road. Here, I learnt why bicycles should not be allowed on the main roads, or at least, I could feel it when a large truck came passed and nearly sucked me in towards the moving vehicle. If you were not cycling at a fast enough speed, sometimes the draught sucked you in a little. This was not a fun experience. If you were travelling at the correct speed, it pushed you along; and by correct speed, I mean the same as the passing vehicles or not far from it. But I didn't think this was for everyone, not that I was an experienced bicycle rider; I enjoy adrenaline.

I kept getting closer to the Balaton Lake. A few teenagers passed; I knew I was on the right path. I asked them for direction. They were on bicycles too and were able to show me where to go exactly. I gave them sweets at the end as a thank-you, only because I had some, not that I went out of my way to buy some for them.

That night, I arrived at Siófok. It was a tough day. It was getting dark, so I continued to cycle for a bit to get myself farther up the road, but it was too dark, and I did not want to risk my life. I cycled past a selection of holiday homes and asked a person if I could place a tent in the grassy area across the road from the house beside a set of railway tracks.

They got their husband. 'We are on holiday here,' they said. Good enough for me; that was enough authority.

Half an hour passed, and I could hear someone calling. 'Are you hungry?' said the voice.

Now this was a tough question for me to answer. Was I hungry? Usually not as I eat throughout the day, but tonight I could eat, and I felt like I needed company. I went over to the family. They were Italian and Hungarian. They were very interested in my travels and provided me with enough Italian pasta to fill my belly and a goody bag for the next few days ahead.

That morning, I was back on the road to travel even farther south. I cycled to a place called Tamási after midday; it was roasting. I had a choice, continue on the road I was on or head right along a different road which would take me farther on. I chose the right.

I cycled for several hours with corn to the right of me and sunflowers to the left. That night, I was aiming for Pecs, seventy kilometres from the border. About sixty kilometres after Tamási, I stopped at a watering hole for a few jars of water. I asked the bartender the temperature that day, thirty-five degrees. It felt like it. I got out the map a few times to have a look. Eventually, it was time to go. Before that, I had asked the bartender how far away Pecs was. 'Forty-five kilometres', they said.

As I left, they were about to shut the watering hole and asked if I wanted a lift. 'Of course, thanks very much,' I replied. I loaded the backpack and bicycle into the van, and they locked the van and started to walk around the corner. I was confused. It turned out they were going around the corner to shut the watering hole for the afternoon.

Thirty kilometres later, it was time to get out. They never did say a lift to Pecs, though thirty kilometres was more than enough. And I was happy to be able to sit down in the comfortable van and watch the countryside go past at much faster speeds than I could cycle. Eventually, I arrived in Pecs after having to climb a reasonably sized steep hill until I got to the top, and it was easy coasting from there. Along the top of the hill, I saw a walker at the side of the road who had a flask of water, and I was in need of some. I gave the person two euros for the flask and happily glided down the hill. For some reason, the water was fairly potent, Hungarian border water.

That night, I was in search of a road to take me easily into Croatia. It got late. I asked someone if they knew where I could find a campsite; they gave great directions, and I was there in no time.

Strange events happened that night. I could not remember going to sleep but awoke at some stage or another and thought I was being transferred in the back of a lorry. Yes, absolute madness. I just thought this. I had arrived late into the campsite and did not pay. I placed my tent on the plot, had that flask of water, and went to sleep. I was wrecked when I arrived, and at one stage, it felt as if I was moving in the tent; hence, I thought I was being transported. I even peeked my head out to see what the craic was, but for some reason, I thought what I thought. But in the end, I came to the conclusion that the wind was shaking the tent; or possibly, it was the neighbours, not that the Hungarian owners had loaded me into a truck while I was sleeping and sent me elsewhere for not informing them I was staying there that night. It was a possibility, but it was not reality.

The next day, I awoke, packed up the tent, and had some food. Within a matter of minutes, I had a Hungarian screaming at me for my passport. I really did not like the situation but eventually gave them my passport, and they wrote me a receipt for the night. I had no Hungarian chips or euros. I had notes but no coins. I left. One day I would send them the three euros they were demanding or stay there again another time and pay double. Some people though. It was understandable —livelihood. But I hated it when people were shouting at me in another language; it sounded like they were so angry and annoyed and very loud for all to hear. Creating a scene for all to see and hear. It was not a fun experience but I was used to it.

I found my road and headed for Croatia, my first border patrol crossing.

CROATIA

This was where I got the first stamp in my passport. On through I went without a hitch. I found a restaurant and had a nice meal and a jar of water before cycling to the place of Našice. Far north-east of Croatia was very easy to cycle, almost similar as the cycling that was had in the Netherlands, with the exception that there were no cycle ways, just roads—excellent. At one stage, it began to rain very heavily, so I decided to find lodgings for the night.

The first hotel I came across was thirty-five euros. No thank you. There must be cheaper ones available in this underdeveloped village. Thirty-five euros was cheap enough for a hotel, but I wanted something cheaper. I found it—twenty euros for one night in a hotel off a main road. I ended up staying there for one and a half nights. I arrived and was shown to my room.

A few hours had passed, and I was asked if I would like some food or if I was hungry. I said no. I was asked again and then once more and decided I would eat the food that the person had prepared.

I went downstairs to a double steak dinner—excellent, what I needed. And I tucked right in. I finished off the two steaks and about half the chips and a tomato. I was only going to eat half but decided to eat all the tomato as it may have been thrown out. The chips, on the other hand, were not natural; they had been processed. I was willing to leave them behind; hopefully, they had a dog.

The next day, I awoke, packed up my belongings, and headed to the watering hole for several jars of high-strength Croatian water. I also had to take care of the bill for the room and to receive my passport. 'That's thirty euros,' said the owner of the hotel. I didn't argue with the person as I had had a powerful hot dinner the night before and was willing to shed ten euros for their cause. I had a few more jars of water and decided it was time for a nap, and away back to bed I went.

That night when I awoke, I was trying to plan my way out. Where was the number fifty-three road? I pondered this throughout the day. This road would take me to

Bosnia and Herzegovina. *I wonder where it is.* I noticed a lot of traffic on the road throughout the night. I opened up an old version of Google Maps on my LG touchscreen, and it turned out that the hotel I was staying at was on the number fifty-three road, very handy.

But yes, I had been carrying this phone that was not a smartphone. However, it did have Wi-Fi connectivity, an Internet browser, a decent camera, and Google Maps pre-installed. This was basically extra weight but served a purpose when there was Wi-Fi.

I slept until about five o'clock in the morning and then left on the road towards Bosnia and Herzegovina. It was about fifty to seventy kilometres before I reached the border. I passed through the small town of Slavonski Brod and used whatever Croatian currency I had left. I still had a few kuna, which was spent on fruit and yoghurt for the day. I then headed towards the direction of Bosnia and Herzegovina.

BOSNIA AND HERZEGOVINA

When I approached the Croatian border, there were many people crossing through. It was quite a number, all passing through for what I assumed was work. I was cycling through, the tourist in a red cap.

It was funny. I was on my bicycle, and all these people were going to work. This was the life for me—for now.

I passed through the border without bother. I even got a stamp in my passport as it was looking rather bare. I then headed for Derventa, where I hoped to find some Internet to respond to various emails and messages—success.

Now I had a big decision to make. Would I head south-west to an unknown place called Banja Luka or continue on the path I was on, heading for the known Sarajevo, and cycle south-east? I decided to head for Banja Luka, mix the cycling up a little, and cut across the country. And I made one of the greatest decisions. It was tough but definitely a good decision. I saw much cutting west, much of the countryside that I may not have seen had I gone the other way. Or it could be the opposite; the other way could have been much worse as it was looking fairly industrial as I cycled from the border. I had thought about changing direction at one stage but the thought of the other route being worse helped me on my way to keep on going.

I eventually arrived to a place about ten kilometres or thirty minutes away from Banja Luka and stopped for some supplies. When I went to pay, I only had euros. I supposed, at the time and still to this day, the country was not part of the European Union. A person in the line offered to exchange. I was hesitant. Eventually, I gave in and accepted twenty marka for ten euros. I thought this was a good deal as I had bought enough food to last me a day or two and had change left over for the future.

I headed towards Banja Luka. A reason I had travelled there was that the other route on the map had a motorway taking you to Sarajevo, and well, I know bicycles cannot cycle there; and again, I would not risk a potential fine or even having the bicycle taken from me. I was unable to search for an alternative route to Sarajevo. The primary information that I had was enough for this solo traveller, and having the bicycle potentially removed for a period would have been the worst outcome. Every other road was okay, even the ones which had a sign of a bicycle in a red circle; I assumed that meant drivers must be vigilant. There was no solid line through, just a bicycle in a red circle. Then there was another road sign similar to the peace sign or a circle split into thirds with a picture of a bicycle, tractor, and livestock.

Again, there was no solid line through to suggest a no-go area.

I decided to take the national road to Banja Luka instead of getting on the highway. I assumed I could do that later on. Eventually, I found my road that would take me directly to Mostar. I would have started on the road at about eight o'clock in the evening. I cycled for a wee while and had something to eat at the side of the road.

The whole way up until this point, I had been cycling through hills and mountains. The road I was on I would call death road considering the amount of roadside plaques and murals of what I assumed were of the people who had lost their lives on this treacherous road, not that it was scary, I was extra careful when I could be. The road reminded me of a road on a *Top Gear* special, but it turned out they never went to Bosnia and Herzegovina. The beautiful road took you right through the Bosnian mountains and canyons. I was amazed at what beautiful scenery I was absorbing. I could only smile at the progress I had made. I had never expected to see such beauty in a country that may not have the greatest historical background. I supported them, and I was glad that I chose this route.

I stopped for food at the side of death road at a safe area with plenty of room. By the time I had finished, I realised how dark it was. At this part of the road, there was a type of rest area—well, I was able to stop there. I could see a large part of the canyon overhanging on the road, and the cars were going right underneath it.

That could break off one day while someone was driving underneath it and could cause a serious fatality. I would avoid the opposite side of the road. I decided I would pull off the road for my own safety and the safety of the people driving their cars as, at night, they were certainly on a mission to get to wherever they were going, overtaking from the other side to the side I was on—scary biscuits. Luckily, I had lights on the bicycle.

I stopped at a house along the road. I could see there were lights on and several people talking. I decided to go over and ask a question. 'How far until the end of the road?' I asked.

'Very far', replied one of them.

For a few minutes, I contemplated if I wanted to start cycling again. I asked if I could place a tent for the night. One of them invited me into their home that had belonged to their late parent that they were renovating and offered me a bed for the night. When we got back to the house, we all had a few jars of water as well as several glasses for good measure as we had all been working that day.

I was shown to a bed which was very comfortable, and after the hundred plus kilometres or so that I had cycled, I needed it. I did not set an alarm that night, which was the usual. I had planned to get up early, but my body was exhausted. I got up whenever I did and was not sure of the time. I thanked the two people who had let me stay in their home. We had a jug of water and breakfast before I departed. I gave more appreciation to the Bosnians and thanked them, and then I headed off down the road, E661, following the river Vrbas.

In the light of day, the road really was beautiful. There would have been cliffs and rock faces of about twenty metres making up the canyon. It was spectacular and something that I may have seen before in a digital medium but still brand new to these eyes. I was amazed. I powered on, going through various tunnels and crossing bridges, all the while following the river Vrbas.

This river had crystal clear water at parts; other parts were covered in rubbish, no joke. This was just where the rubbish had happened to be caught. I am sure all rivers are the same. Many times, I wanted to swim but was unable to as I was cycling; plus, there was no easy way down. It was hot enough that day, but I was trying to cover distance. I was able to bask like a lizard in the sun and enjoy the natural beauty. Swimming can wait until I reach the Mediterranean Sea, if I head down that direction.

I continued forwards, passing small village after small village, until I reached a place called Jajce or Donji Vakuf; I was near sure it was Jajce. There were signs for a waterfall. As I was passing on the road, I could see the waterfall; therefore, there was no need to have a closer inspection of the tourist attraction. I was tempted, but I had already seen it from the road.

Forwards I went into Bugojno. Here, I took a wrong turn, which was on the way to Split on the Croatian coast. Must have been the jars of water from the previous night. I looked at my European road map and then decided to go across the street to ask a family how I would get back on the road to Mostar. The road was not far; they explained it well.

They asked if I wanted some fruit. 'Yes, that'd be lovely on this very warm day,' I replied. Someone understood, and I was presented with food. Then I was asked if I would like some dinner. Again, I said yes as I was rather famished. Not often you get spoilt like that. I enjoyed the time with the family, the food they provided me with and thanked them for having me as a guest. They were amazed and interested about why I was in their country and asked many other questions, which I happily answered, and one translated to the rest. Everyone was bewildered.

I was redirected back to the road and began to cycle again. For about twenty kilometres, it was smooth; then all of a sudden, I was presented with a large mountain to climb to progress. It was getting later and later. The sky was as clear as transparent glass. I decided to take a rest halfway up the large hill at a picnic area. I met some local Bosnians there who drove a rather nice Beemer. They spoke a reasonable level of english and were a bit of craic. We shared a flask of water together and then parted ways. They were able to transfer water into my flask as I had little to none; I appreciated this.

After they had left, a wild kitten appeared and was walking about the same area, meowing and looking for something to eat. I decided I would take the kitten. When I began to stroke the cat, it began to purr and seemed very happy and content. I then put the kitten in the neck of my jersey and began to walk about with it, but it started to cry, and I did not like the sound of this. I then took the kitten out and put it on the floor to try to gain its trust. The kitten was having none of it. I decided to leave it, even though I knew I probably could have provided a better life than it was having. Who knew? Maybe the cat was very happy and content where it was; that was its home. Who was I to take a kitten from the wild? But to take an animal out of its natural surroundings could be very stressful. I really wanted to take the kitten, but it did not want to go with me; we parted ways. There goes a broken heart.

I continued to climb and climb. It was getting later, the whole sky was lit up with the stars, and it was magical. Never had I seen that many stars. I noticed an object in the sky moving at a steady speed that was not an aeroplane, which reminded me of people who believe in aliens. Madness. I was happy to have the unknown. That night, I saw my first shooting star.

I was on the road to Prozor. Along the journey, I decided it was time to call it a night and called to the door of a house about halfway down the other side of the hill. At the house, I asked if I could place a tent in the yard until morning. A person answered the door; a young person there had to translate. They mediated a conversation, and I was invited into their home, which had their family and friends. I was the unexpected guest. I didn't know what was expected of a guest except common courtesy. Language was a barrier, and I wasn't going to dance like a monkey; I really should have.

I was given several biscuits, chocolates, and multiple jugs of water. Then I was shown to a guest house which had a number of rooms, and I was the only occupant. I had not expected this. Here, I was able to have a shower after a few days on the trot and prepare for the next day with a good night's sleep. Before bed, I had a flask of water, looked up at the clear sky, and was ready for sleep.

I headed for the town of Mostar that morning. On the road I went. Luckily, I had chosen a house which was halfway down the hill as at least, when I was ready to leave, I would have a hill start to help me glide down the road at speed. Through the town of Jablanica I went and onto the main road for Mostar. There was nothing really that eventful, just an enjoyable cycle through the mountains next to the river Vrbas. Eventually, I was within a five-kilometre radius, and I received the first puncture of my travels several weeks into this venture.

On week two or three, I had lost my pump, puncture repair kit, and tools, which were stolen during my time in the Netherlands and Germany. In the Czech Republic, a rather snide person asked why I had not replaced them. *Well, to be honest, I prefer to suffer in silence and deal with a problem when it arises.* Anyway, it was the first puncture since I started. I quickly removed the wheel, got out the spare tube, and tried to insert that into the rim; unfortunately, the valve was too big for the rim, which was built for a Presta valve. I had a Shrader valve in my hand. I then stopped a cyclist on the road who was going the opposite way and asked them if I could use their pump. Several minutes passed, and I thanked them. Another five minutes, and the tyre was flat, a proper puncture. There was nothing I could do but continue to walk the remaining kilometres. I reached the city of Mostar.

When I arrived, I asked someone in the street on a bicycle if they knew where I could find a bicycle shop. They were happy to help, drew me a map, and explained the route to the shop. I went to the repair hut and got a Presta valve tube, which they gave me free of charge. I gave them the Shrader valve tube that I had and was not able to use. They smiled. I thanked them and headed off around the city.

I came across the Stari Most Bridge, and I never jumped off it, maybe next time.

One reason I would not jump was that I had all my belongings up there, including passport, and all it takes is one person to walk away with it, the opportunist. After leaving Mostar, I found accommodation in a small village nearby to rest and recover.

I left the small village outside Mostar happy but a little lost. I had just been fed and watered for almost a week without much exercise. Where was I to go?

From the village, I managed to secure a lift on a bus to Dubrovnik from the accommodation. Well, fifteen kilometres outside the city limits of Dubrovnik was not bad. It would have saved two hundred kilometres worth of cycling. On the bus there was much sandy and watery scenery blurring by; this would have been tough in this heat, with the Croatian sun beaming down, though when you wake up early, you can get plenty of ground covered.

Luckily, I did not have to cycle and was travelling at a cool hundred kilometres per hour or so. Sitting on a bus or any sort of moving vehicle was just a great feeling when you have been cycling and pushing yourself. You moved, and the world stood still. You had a seat between you and the road similar to a bicycle but at a much faster speed. Yes, very convenient, especially if you were not driving. When you have been cycling the last few weeks, it can be good to have a rest and let the views go by, have a think, and enjoy the movement. When cycling, you do the work; you are the driver.

The bus stopped; the journey ended. Out I went into the midday heat, with a bunch of people watching my movement. *Best to go downhill*, I thought, *before making a start uphill on the national road.* To a cafe I went to see about the use of Wi-Fi to quickly map the journey and to see where exactly I was on the road and how far it was to the border of Montenegro.

When cycling, though, do you have to be prepared? Mentally and physically? Was all that gear necessary? Or were you sufficient with yourself? If you were to type 'cycling person', into your search-engine you would probably get all these people covered in Lycra and skintight clothing promoting and feeding the cycling market. Really though, is cycling about being aerodynamic or about clean mechanical fun?

When cycling, you choose which roads you are taking, you choose where you are going, and you should know the correct way. But there are times when we take a wrong turn by accident due to human error, and we find ourselves a little lost. It is best to backtrack when that happens.

Off the bus, I pedalled downhill. I went into the cafe and quickly mapped where I was and where I was going. It was a straight road; now I was aware of the distance.

When you have rested for a number of days and have sat on a bus for two hours, you need to prepare in whatever way you feel is right to mentally be ready. Have a drink of water, map your ride, check your tyres, or all of the above. At least you cannot fault what you have checked beforehand. Anyway, all was well. If I stayed on this road, I would be there in a short period. Thank you to the driver and the donation of the ticket.

Off I went after my water. As I may have said before, any journey that starts uphill is a journey that I would avoid. This was not the case in this instance as this was the route that would take me to Montenegro. This hill was different, a small incline which was more intense. But I did see a couple tackle the hill, and they were probably younger than I was. This was from the view of the cafe, though they did not have any luggage. A leisurely cycle for them.

At the cafe, I had asked if there were any caps, using the translator I had acquired during my time in Mostar for fairly cheap. 'Bole kape?' I said, looking at the screen. They seemed to understand that I was looking for a cap and directed me to the coat rack, and success, there was a cap—a cap that would shield my face from the blazing midday sun. It didn't really fit very well, a tight one, but did the job to protect my face.

Off I went up the hill, pedalling; everything was great. At the top of the hill, it was fairly easy coasting. It was almost like any other road except it was on the Croatian coast and nothing like the road to Würzburg through the German hills. That was not a heavenly ride but it was not impossible. I arrived to the border of Montenegro.

MONTENEGRO

I was wearing a Croatian football jersey. I decided to turn the jersey inside out as a personal sign of respect towards the people of Montenegro. The police at the border understood, but I think they would have preferred it if I took it off and burnt it or at least changed it completely. I did this out of respect for a new nation of people. I knew nothing about them apart from them participating in the World Cup in months previous. I basically wore that Croatian top for a total of a few hours. I should have bought a league jersey instead of an international team to avoid any confrontation. Who knew what to expect as you went farther east? The media has us fairly worked up about the east.

Sun still blazing high in the sky, I progressed farther south-east. It was going to get much warmer. The first resort I passed by was in Herceg Novi, a seaside town with a reasonable-sized boat dock, large enough beach, and the Adriatic Sea. Croatia had this, but there was little sand that I saw, though I only really experienced about twenty kilometres of Croatian coast, and this was mostly cliffs. There was not much else to say about Herceg Novi.

I had some croissants from the area of rest in Mostar. I had taken many. There was a stray dog walking around the place sniffing, and I thought it was looking something to eat. I ripped off a piece of a croissant and gave it to the dog.

The dog looked at it, sniffed it, and walked away. Wild stray dogs only want meat, or maybe the croissant was not of the best quality or the ingredients not organically sourced, and it knew this. But no, they prefer meat, but I had none.

I followed the sea as far as I could before coming across a tourist information kiosk. Well, I had seen a ferry crossing first, which led me to the kiosk. I asked where the ferry was going. It turned out the ferry was going to cut across the peninsula and to the opposite side.

This would reduce the coastal cycling forty kilometres. Every little helps. The cost of the ferry service was only a euro for a bicycle. To Kotor I went with the bicycle.

From Kotor, I headed to Budva, following the signs as I went, since I entered the country. I eventually reached Budva. Some cycling was done that day, up and down some rather large hills, not that it was a nightmare to get to; it was frustrating travelling through the massive hills, and it was not easy by bicycle. People may even say that it was slightly dangerous as the traffic was fairly close to the edge. I reached the top of the highest hill I had climbed the whole day and zoomed all the way down into Budva. This was necessary to progress. But I supposed I could have gone a different route, but I chose this coastal one.

It was a very busy town, even on a Sunday, full of tourists and holidaymakers. I randomly came across two local people. I asked them if they had a flask of water as I was in need of something to drink. They decided to show me around the town. Off we went. There was not much to see in a seaside town, but I was shown old town and new town. New town was full of tourists, souvenir shops, and watering holes. Old town was cobbled streets and tight alleyways which led you through a castle-like structure.

I was getting bored. I asked them if there were any places to cliff dive. They spoke in their local language. Then there was a yes. 'There are several places,' one of them said.

'Let's go,' I replied.

We walked. It was about a ten-minute walk along the coastline, eventually reaching a cliff we could jump off. I went into the water first to roughly be the same temperature as the water. They told me that they were about five, seven, and ten metres high. *Okay*, I thought. We started with the smallest one first, the five metres. It looked very dangerous. I could see rocks among the seabed which obviously looked closer than they actually were.

'You can go first,' I said to them. Off they jumped, an elegant dive.

Here goes something. I dived, excellent. When I had jumped, I noticed the error in my entry into the water as I nearly scraped my nose off the rocks at the bottom. I wouldn't be doing that again.

Something was missing—a platform to run off and dive, instead of the cliff edge. A few more jumps, and we were onto the next one. Again, we walked farther on around the coastline. I could see the cliffs in the distance. These were the cliffs. 'That is seven metres,' they said.

'All right', I replied.

Now this one was a flat rock to have a bit of a run up. Again, this looked dangerous but sure when in Budva. To reassure me, they jumped in feet first. It was my time to jump. After deep breaths and a look at the sky, I was golden. *Here goes something again.* I took a decent run up, and off the cliff I went, with hands in first and then the feet, a dive. The second one was sweet. On their first dive, they went with head and legs in at the same time. They had hurt themselves, or at the very least, it looked painful to watch. I hurt my wrist, so I decided to call it a day as I did not want to hurt it any further. I had cycling to be doing later on.

The third jump, which was much higher and a bit of a trek to get to, looked the most dangerous; there was even a plaque in memorial of a diver who had lost their life diving from that ledge. I would save that one for later in life. Looking back, I wished I had jumped off that cliff. But I was looking to cliff dive, and that was what I did that evening. No need to go too extreme.

That night, they decided to take me out on a night out in Budva. I wished I had not stayed for several reasons. It was catered for average tourists and had poor taste, average club music, and many, many lights. At one stage, I thought my eyes were deceiving me. I thought Budva, Montenegro, experienced the Northern Lights. No, they were just spotlights high in the sky.

Several hours passed, and I called it a night. We headed off on our own separate ways. But at least I gained knowledge of where I can cliff dive in Budva if I ever returned there and this would be one reason to return. I found a campsite and camped for the night with the hope of reaching Albania by evening the next day. I had arrived late at the campsite and had set up camp without paying, easy going. Before bed, I checked the third tablet that I had. Well, the crystalline screen had basically burst, and the screen was cracked; therefore, it was rendered broken.

That morning, I awoke to the heat of the sun penetrating through the single-layered tent. It was time to get up. It was not very comfortable to be in a tent when it was roasting. Well, my tent was not catered for that sort of heat. I packed up my gear and headed off down and up the road. At this stage, I was following the coast of Montenegro towards the Albanian border.

Along the way, I passed a town where I was able to buy lunch and whatnot. In a supermarket, I paid twenty-nine cents for a Snickers bar. Why on earth do we pay three times that back home is beyond me. Powerful stuff. I should have stocked up but did not on the unhealthy treats, which would be no good in the sun.

Before I left the town, I thought about bringing the tablet to a repair shop to fix the cracked screen and digitiser as they were completely broken. It was basically useless. I went in search of a repair shop to see if I could get it fixed cheaply and quickly. No such luck. They would not touch it or waste their time trying to fix it as it was not a branded tablet, such as a Samsung, which they were most familiar with. I had a look around, and the cheapest one

I could find was for sixty-five euros. I pondered and was very tempted. *Fourth tablet on my travels, would it be worth it?* The answer would be yes, but I never purchased.

I made lunch and had a mini sleep on the beach. It was enjoyable, but there was too much sand being blown about. I called it a day and headed towards what I thought was the exit but turned out to be a nudist beach. Today was not the day for the beach, maybe earlier in the day but not when I arrived.

I found my way back to the exit and asked a few questions about the Albanian border and was told that I could not follow the coast any further as there was the river Bojana to cross—good information. I would have to head back the way I came. I cycled twenty kilometres for nothing. After lunch and a quick dip in the sea, off I headed down the same road as earlier. I just powered on through; I had to. In time, it would be dark, not that that had affected me at all during my travels.

I had not really accomplished much that day, plenty of cycling about and indecisive malarkey. I was in no hurry. I came to a supermarket where I was able to stock up on supplies. When I was rearranging my bicycle, a few tanned children came up to me and demanded I give them some of my juice. When I say 'demanded', the group came out of nowhere and came over waving their hands and expected a drink. They wanted to drink from the bottle. No thank you. I don't know what diseases you could possess. I jest, of course. I told them to put their heads back, and I would pour the juice in. The three of them fell in line and held their heads back, and I shared the juice amongst them. They then returned to their family.

I was on the road again. I was heading for the Albanian border, and I was on the correct road this time for sure. Along the journey, I needed more water. I stopped at a house and used a hosepipe.

Hopefully, this water was safe to drink. A passer-by had asked if I needed help. 'No thank you, though thank you for the offer,' I said.

Several kilometres later, I felt the bicycle beginning to lag. *Oh no*, I thought, *it's going to be a puncture.* And it was. Luckily, I had a spare tube. I quickly changed the tyre. A few people beeped their horns while I was at the side of the road. I was unsure why, but I assumed it was due to the cowboy hat I was wearing or maybe the fact that I had a flat tyre and was changing. I didn't know but responded appropriately.

Onwards I progressed up and down through the Montenegrin mountains, eventually coming to a main road that would take me to the border. I came across two Albanians who had come across the border, I assumed legally, but their path was well out of way, or maybe they were from Montenegro and were hanging about in the bushes. We had some chat, and then I was on my way.

There was a supermarket, a fancy large one, probably to give the Montenegrin people their final meal or the Albanians their first meal. Anyway, I rolled in. I assumed I looked like a traveller or something foreign as I got many strange looks from the staff. It was all good though, and well, I was a foreigner, and I was on a mission. I had no time to please everyone. I picked up some more supplies and left the shop. I had a large yoghurt before departing. I headed down past the front of the shop to use the rubbish bin—you know, normally. The manager came out to have a look and probably thought the foreigner was up to no good. No, just using the bin like a good traveller.

I departed from the supermarket, off down the road this time. Several kilometres and many lorries later, I reached the border, ready to cross. Bright lights were everywhere. *Onto the next one*, I thought. I underwent the usual procedure—passport check. As I was passing through, I began speaking to a Russian who was also crossing. Now the Albanian border police were giving them a hard time when crossing through. They were through, and so was I.

The police then stopped them, checked their passport, and looked through their belongings. They then demanded to see some money from the Russian. They wanted to see fifty euros. I thought this was funny as there was a handshake at the start of the conversation. Maybe they were just being friendly; I myself would not be this responsive.

Anyway, the Russian then asked to borrow some money. I was reluctant. The next happening was weird. They had asked for my passport in exchange of their bank card. I was supposed to find a cash machine and withdraw money from it. 'No deal', I said.

They had a laptop. For security purposes, I said that I would give them the fifty euros to mind the laptop until they returned my money. They understood and complied. Fifty euros was in their hand and the laptop in my backpack. The police were baffled.

'Are you selling that for fifty euros?' the police said.

'You got to do what you got to do,' said the Russian.

At this stage, I thought the laptop was mine.

We headed into Albania about twenty metres, found a cafe, and had an Albanian jug of water. The Russian returned the euros, and I returned the laptop. They asked where I would be sleeping that night. I said I would continue to cycle another few kilometres. 'Are you crazy? What about the gangsters and the bad people?' they said.

'What are you on about?' I said with a strange look on my face.

'It's a dangerous country. You have to be careful,' they replied.

I had a think and thought it would be best to listen to the Russian. Who knew what lay beyond the Albanian border late at night? I did not. There were no street lights or anything, just pure darkness. This was how it usually was at the border though. I decided to listen and made the decision to stay on the border of Montenegro before departing in the morning. We finished our jugs of water and headed back to Montenegro. They also advised that I leave my bicycle at the cafe. Again, I was very reluctant, but I left my bicycle there, locked up for the night, the chain only around the frame. I should have removed the front wheel and attached the chain through the front wheel, back wheel, and frame, though there was a certain level of security at the cafe/restaurant. I didn't ask many questions; all I knew was that I would be staying somewhere on the border close to Albania.

We arrived at an abandoned petrol station after crossing the border. They collected some clothing they had washed previously, I assumed, and left them to dry in the natural heat.

We then headed around the back and up a set of stairs. 'You want the bed or the floor?' they asked. I opted for the floor. This was their temporary home. They had found it; it was their's. It would have been rude if I were to take the bed. It wasn't mine. I would be happy on the floor instead of out in Albania with the gangsters who could maybe steal my precious bicycle or even worse.

They closed the door, and I got ready for bed. I was brushing my teeth. 'Do you need water?' they asked.

'Actually, yes, I do,' I replied.

'Here you go,' they responded.

I rolled out my sleeping bag and got in. I decided to wear a mosquito head net as I slept to protect me from any insects that were about. Throughout the night, it felt as if there were insects in my sleeping bag. Now this could have just been the hair from my leg rubbing against the sleeping bag. It did not feel right. I slept the night. I was not one who can lie on a floor with my hands by my side and sleep, so the arms were out of the sleeping bag on the wooden floor. This was probably not wise, but I could not sleep otherwise.

The next morning, I woke up and felt itchy. I went outside for my morning stretch, and the sun was blazing, too hot for comfort. I turned around and noticed a wasp's nest right on the arch of the doorway.

I did not panic, but I bloody hate wasps. Ever since a young child, I was their enemy. When I looked, I was sure they saw blood dropping in my cheeks, and a few attacked me—you know, just flew after me. I threw windmills around the place to clear them from my personal space. I did not look back until I was ready to go in. They got back to their business, and I got back to my packing.

The Russian had gone out to look for gas for their stove so we could have a jug of water, no luck finding a canister. We then had breakfast and headed back into Albania for a final jug of water. At the border, we had more trouble. The police took them into a separate room, and I assumed they questioned them. Thirty minutes or so had passed, and they were free to go into the country.

As time passed, I began to think about leaving as I was in a hurry, sort of, not really. It was nearly ten o'clock, and well, cycling in the midday heat was no good for the body but had to be done when you were moving and wanted to clear distance. I decided to stay as I thought about how the French Mexican person cleared off without saying a thing. This was not how I rolled. I waited until they were free to enter the country.

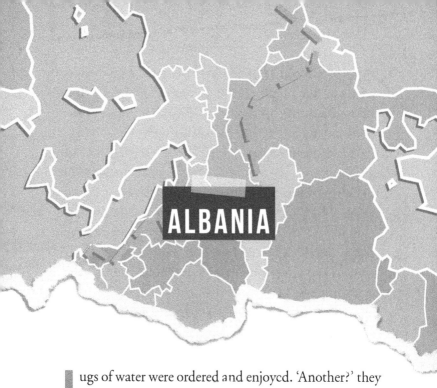

ALBANIA

J ugs of water were ordered and enjoyed. 'Another?' they asked. Another was had.

I then had a look at my bicycle and saw another flat tyre. This was not ideal. I had changed the tube yesterday. I tried to pump the tyre up some more in the hope that it was not burst—no luck. I then removed the tube and fixed the puncture. This took a while as the pump I used was not great; plus, the puncture was releasing small amounts of air with every pump. I then decided to fix my spare tube as well, if there were any more punctures along the way, I would be prepared for the road ahead as any fatalities could be remedied quickly and efficiently.

Time progressed, and it was getting closer to midday. I was ready to get on the road. Tubes were fixed, and I was on the road again. Before leaving, the Russian had said that they needed money and was willing to sell their laptop for fifty euros. Without hesitation, I gave them the money for the laptop. It would be handy in my travels for communicational purposes, excellent. We left the cafe, shook hands, and wished each other well.

As we were leaving, a number of children came over, demanding money, not that I found this annoying, but they surrounded me. 'Money, money, money', they said repeatedly. I had no change and couldn't exactly give them a ten each. I thought they were maybe attracted to the bicycle and thought that I was somebody with disposable money. I was a traveller. I was travelling.

Please leave me alone and do not demand. Very rude, I thought. And had they been more polite, I doubt I would have given them any as I was trying to look after myself. Then at the same time if I had coins it would have been a different matter.

We departed in separate directions. I headed into Albania in the sunlight. No need to worry about gangsters now; they were all sleeping. It was the safest option for Albania. I must have cycled thirty kilometres in the midday heat before making my first stop for a break at an abandoned petrol station.

Here, there was a brute of a person and their young child. That was the only way to describe them. I had a drink of water. I saw many chickens about and watermelons. The person then headed into the abandoned shed, which could be their home; grabbed a watermelon; and signalled if I would like some. I nodded. I then got my knife and began slicing the watermelon in half as I would see what I could eat first before slicing it all up. I love watermelon, one of the nicest fruits in my opinion.

It was sweet and contained water. What more could you want on a hot day? I continued to eat, throwing the skins to the chickens to finish off. I didn't know chickens ate watermelon, but they do. I then went to my backpack and made a meaty sandwich with cheese to give to the person and child. They were grateful, and I was grateful for the watermelon.

A person then pulled up in their yellow dump truck with an empty trailer. I asked them where they were going. 'Tirana', they answered.

I checked my map. 'Can you give me a lift to Tirana?' I replied, lifting my bicycle and backpack.

We finished our food and loaded on my bicycle. I kept my backpack with me as this contained all my most important valuables, such as money and passport and the necessities that I would need for travelling. Without these, it would be a much different type of travelling. Off to Tirana we went, seventy kilometres of highway on and off. As we were driving, they offered me a jar of water that was staying cool inside a polystyrene container. *Very smart*, I thought, and it was surprisingly cold, considering it was very hot outside. It felt very relaxing to be sitting in a moving vehicle, taking in the natural surroundings and beauty of a country. If you were on a bicycle and going downhill, that was more enjoyable.

An hour or so passed, and we arrived outside Tirana, about five kilometres. They parked up the truck at the side of the road, and it was time for me to depart. My bicycle was unloaded from the trailer, and they explained that the best way to get me through Albania was to look for signs, pointing to their eyes. I understood. 'Elbasan', they said. We shook hands, and off they went.

I then enjoyed a Snickers at the side of the road for some extra calories in the heat and headed off into the centre of Tirana. The first thing on the agenda was to find some Wi-Fi to inform my family of my current location. I went to several cafes before being directed to a fancy-looking watering hole with Wi-Fi.

Before leaving a shanty cafe, a young child went 'Tourista'. I laughed and explained to them that I was no *tourista*. They probably could not understand this concept, but I had to correct them as I was no tourist. I was touring. Anyway, off to the watering hole I went for a jug of water. I opened the laptop and started it up, and it was in Russian. I used my LG touchscreen phone to see if I could change the language using the results from Google—no luck.

I tried to connect to the Wi-Fi. It was fairly standard—password, repeat password. It did not work, but the Internet on my phone was working; unfortunately, it was not Android. I finished my coffee and decided I would find a computer service centre. I came across one with a rather attractive counter person who happened to know nothing about computers and was constantly ringing their friend or boss to see if they could fix the laptop or at least reinstall Windows—no luck. I left in search of another shop. Around the corner was another. I left the laptop with the person; they said to give them ten minutes. I went and found a cafe to wait while the repair was happening. I went back ten minutes later, and they had tried what I was trying to do in the first cafe that I went to—change the language.

'I can install Windows XP or 7,' they said.

'Windows 7', I said happily.

They then asked if I would like another stick of RAM in the computer. I thought about it, and of course, I would. 'Leave it with me,' they said.

'Excellent', I responded. I went around the corner to a coffee shop to write in my books. I checked my emails and communicated with those back home and afar. The waitress then took money for the jug of water. I gave them five euros, and they gave me back two hundred lekë. I kind of looked at them, like, *Are you serious?* Though I had no idea what the currency rate was, I probably should have checked that on the phone. I left it at that. I then went to my water bottle and asked them if they would fill it. They did and asked if I would like a sandwich of ham and cheese. Of course, I did. Munch. Nice person really.

I went back to the repair shop. 'Another ten minutes', they said.

'Can I use this computer?' I asked.

'Okay', they responded while pointing to a seat.

I then planned on how I would get to the place of Elbasan and farther. It wasn't too hard to locate a way forwards. With the help of the Albanian person who reminded me to open my eyes and to look for the signs, I had located one upon entry to the city, the capital.

It was not that the person had informed me to open my eyes; it was nice to be told and shown using the hands.

The computer was fixed and ready to go, twenty euros for the service and extra stick of RAM. I packed up my backpack and headed off into the city to head on the road for Elbasan. By this time, it was starting to get dark; it must have been about half past eight at night. I turned on the lights on the bicycle and began cycling. Goodbye, Tirana. It has been brief.

Through the centre in the evening traffic, it was dangerous. Cars were driving about everywhere, not giving a care in the world for pedestrians, cyclists, or passing cars—absolute chaos. It was great craic and an experience. I enjoyed navigating through the traffic system. I was showing aggression now and again when I had to, to warn other vehicles that I was on the road, not a cyclist but a person on a bicycle. It was fun, though not for the faint-hearted.

Eventually, I escaped out of the traffic and onto the road for Elbasan. This was a tough road with several stops. I had some tea and chat with local people who hated their country. I stopped at a petrol station to have some water. There were a few Albanians there who were working. 'What do you think of our country?' they asked.

'It's okay,' I said. From my perspective, it was a beautiful land. They laughed and told me how much they hated it, and if they could, they would leave. I could understand. I could never live my whole life there, but I would give it a chance. Plus, you were born where you were born; you had no choice in that matter. Passing through, I enjoyed it but mostly from the seat of a lorry, taking in the scenic views which were new to me, such as the Albanian mountains. This was life to them.

I shook hands with them and cycled into the darkness. I climbed and climbed, eventually calling it a night when I found a nice place to camp off the road to Elbasan. I would finish the other ten kilometres in the morning. With the tent set up and teeth brushed, it was time for bed. The sleep was good. Pity the rocks were protruding through the under layer. Therefore, it was not the best place to camp; but at the time, it was.

That morning, I awoke to the sound of someone outside my tent walking about. Up I lept to have a peek at what was there. Out I popped my head to see a small child lingering about the tent and walking about the plain with a bucket. I immediately thought they were feeding some livestock, chickens or something. They spoke a reasonable level of english, enough for me to buy them breakfast. 'Tourist?' they asked politely.

'No, not a tourist, traveller', I replied.

'This is my land,' they said.

All right, I thought, *no bother, good for you*. Best to let them think they were in charge, definitely not out of fear but to play along with their game. I let the Albanian have the authority. This was definitely not my land, and I was happy to move on. It could have been worse!

They asked if I was hungry and informed me of a restaurant they knew about. I found this funny because they were very young and knew of a decent restaurant. We headed off for breakfast. It was the best thing for the both of us. We went to the restaurant at the side of the road that I had been cycling the previous night and had breakfast—some meat and some rice, perfect food for the start of the day. The chef in the back didn't look much older than the Albanian I was with. We ate and parted ways.

Before this, I asked them what the bucket was for; they said it was to collect fruit. Then I asked them if they preferred what we had for breakfast or fruit. They preferred the breakfast we had, which was obvious. They scoffed it down as did I. Good deed for the day.

I set off on the road again towards Elbasan. Eventually, the road led me into a developed road that tunnelled through a mountain. I wasn't sure if I could go through but went through anyway. I loved these roads and highways so much, especially when there was a small downward decline. Speed can be had, and distance can be covered. Through the tunnel I went and towards Elbasan. I glided like an aerodynamic piece of matter on the smooth roads.

I arrived, and I found a hotel which had Wi-Fi. I had a jug of water and tried to connect to the Wi-Fi with no such luck. Again, I used five euros to pay; this time, I received five hundred lekë in change. The person the previous day had obviously taken a nice wee tip though I did get a sandwich out of them in the end. Fair play to them, though the money I had was for myself.

I finished my coffee. On the way in, I noticed a large fountain or water feature which looked very appealing to me as I could have had a very quick shower to cleanse myself in the Albanian outdoors. I decided not to, unfortunately, and got back on the road. Pity I didn't. That could have been amusing for the Albanian people— and myself.

I had a quick stop for a water beforehand, and I was on the road again. I proceeded towards Albania in the blistering heat, which was nearly reaching a peak due to the midday coming up. I continued through the Albanian mountains. It was a tough cycle. I wasn't having a good time. I stopped off at a market for supplies in the middle of the mountain—no bread or meat. I got three eggs, a glass, and fruit juice. I then cracked the eggs into the glass and added some fruit juice and then added some sugar to make it even sweeter.

As I was sitting outside the market at a selection of tables and chairs in the shade, a small child appeared out of nowhere, they hung around. I had another drink and gave the child the bottle. I then refilled my water bottle. By the time I got back, they were gone. I assumed they went back to their house to bring to their family the juice they had just got off the *tourista*.

While I sat there, I noticed two small children bringing cattle from one area to another. This made me think about how everyone in Albania and afar had a place in society. I was near sure it was a weekday, and these children were basically farming, working with animals about five times their size; there were no adults in sight. Surely, they should have had school!

Onwards and upwards I went up more hills. I saw a van coming and put my left thumb out as I was cycling, and they pulled over. I put my bicycle in the back of the van and enjoyed the visuals provided by the mountains. We reached a small village where I was able to pick up bread and other supplies for the rest of the day ahead. I had my lunch out the front of the market on the table provided. People were interested in the traveller, but I wasn't interested in them as my morale was low, not too sure why, but it may have been because there was a swarm of them surrounding. Getting ahead of myself but reminded me of my arrival to Mumbai, India…

It was time to set off again. The bicycle was lagging; I was lagging. Happily, another person in their van— well, a taxi bus—pulled over. In the bicycle went, and so did I. Off we went to another small village some twenty kilometres up the road. Here, taxi drivers were asking me where I wanted to go. I would have happily paid; I even went looking for a cash machine but didn't find one—thankfully.

Thus far, the only transport I have paid for has been the one from Ireland to Scotland to Netherlands for a total cost of around seventy pound sterling.

I continued as I knew that I would not be able to get a lift for free this time. Eventually, I came to a petrol station where I had lunch to get my energy levels up for the final push up the Albanian mountains. As I ate a sandwich I had prepared, I could feel something hard inside the sandwich, and I wasn't quite sure what it was. It was foreign and should not have been there. I decided to check out what was inside my mouth and spat the chewed sandwich into my hand to have a wee poke about. It was a piece of my tooth. Crazy Albanian bread and unknown meat, what have you done to my precious tooth?

Farther up the road, I could see what was in front of me. It was going to be tough; a massive mountain was in my face. As I cycled, I was getting a lot of attention from the locals; it was funny even for myself as probably they did not often see people attacking their mountain, or maybe I was different, seeing as I had a backpack and not the standard panniers that you do see. Remarks were made. They had a tourist on their hands on their land. An owner of a local watering hole invited me over for a jug of water. They were a bit of craic, having a joke and a laugh. They were amazed I had cycled from Amsterdam and at the fact I was from the North of Ireland. Hands were shook, and I departed up the hill.

At one stage, I noticed that I could cut across a field which would cut out a few kilometres. I pulled off the road and continued through the field. All I could think about was receiving a puncture. I reached the top of the hill, and lo and behold, I had a flat tyre. Luckily, I had a spare tube in the backpack and quickly sorted the wheel out, though I took my time. Then I had a choice: I could either go to Macedonia or straight through Albania. Two people had advised I go through Albania; they were Albanian. It was a quick decision, and I decided to stay on Albanian soil; it had been good here—well, it had not been bad.

Here, I could see signs for Korçë and Pogradec. These were places that I had heard of throughout the day. Korçë was the place where I could cross from Albania to Greece. Down the other side of the mountain I went, coasting along like a leaf caught in the wind. I could see a large lake in the distance. I had no time to swim; plus, it was after the midday heat, so I probably would have gotten cold afterwards, and I didn't want that. All I wanted was out of Albania.

While I was passing the lake, I saw a person of about the same age; we got chatting, and they gave me a flask of water for the road—sound person. I saw a few campsites along the way and thought about how great it would be to sleep. I moved forwards.

At this stage, my right leg towards the hip began to hurt a little; to not prolong the pain, I decided to get off the bicycle and the left thumb out. Several cars passed. A person in a large red van pulled over. We talked. I signalled I wanted to go forwards as far as possible. They mentioned Korçë. I gave a thumbs up. They then decided they wouldn't give me a lift anymore. *Strange*, I thought.

They then drove about ten metres, got out of the van, and opened the back doors of the van which was filled to the brim with boxes. I thought, *how is my bicycle going to fit in here?* We rearranged some boxes until the bicycle fitted. There were several boxes which did not fit in afterwards because of the space the bicycle had taken. I pointed to the boxes. They waved their finger like they did not care about a few boxes. I put them in beside me in the van.

We then drove through Pogradec, a busy enough town on a Wednesday evening, though there was nothing really to see, another busy place. We progressed onwards. I enjoyed the view from the passenger seat. I felt like a dog but after all the cycling that had been done over the last few months, it was enjoyable to be able to sit and cover much terrain while another machine did the work.

They asked if I would like a jug of water. I said yes. We stopped at a cafe. I noticed a Mercedes pulling up and three police people getting out and walking slowly past the van. The driver and the police chatted. All good. Water was finished, and onwards we went.

They drove me to a petrol station, stopped, and pointed me on the road towards Greece. We shook hands and went our separate ways. They even gave me a pair of gloves for working with the bicycle. They were a good person.

Onwards, I went cycling. At this stage, I needed Wi-Fi to see exactly where I was. I called at a hotel and restaurant. There was a person out the front. 'You need room?' they asked.

'No, just Wi-Fi', I replied.

'Around the back', they said.

Around I went. They followed and showed me a room. 'Twenty euros', they said.

'No thank you,' I said happily. I explained to them that it was too early for me to think about sleep. I thanked them for their approach and left.

I arrived in a place called Bilisht, one of the closest towns to the Korçë border crossing. Here, I found Wi-Fi and found exactly where I was. Onwards I went towards the border. Eventually, I could see the lights of the border control—excellent. I then proceeded through the first passport check. It was no bother.

GREECE

then went through the second checkpoint, the Greek patrol. One of the officers mentioned various illegal substances. 'No thank you,' I replied.

'No, empty your bag,' they said forcefully.

'Oh, right', I said. I then took out my supplies and sleeping bag.

'That's enough,' they said. They only wanted to see what I had in my backpack to see if I was an authentic traveller, and I pretty much proved this by pulling out food and a sleeping bag from my backpack.

'Where can I camp in Greece?' I decided to ask.

'You can camp anywhere,' they said. That was what I wanted to hear, being told by authority that I can camp anywhere. Great success. Welcome to Greece.

I cycled another ten kilometres before finding a place to camp, a field. I set up camp. I had a flask of Albanian water, and as I was lying on my back in the tent, looking up at the sky and the stars, I saw a dog, or maybe it was a horse. No, it was a dog that I saw, the Canis Major apparently.

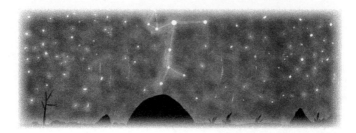

What was important was that I had come across a constellation that I had never seen before, and this was crystal clear. Three stars made up the head, and the rest outlined the body. This was a new experience. This was what I wanted to see, something that I had never seen before.

Then something clicked. The Albanian who gave me a lift in the red van could have been transporting contraband. All of a sudden, I had the notion that they could have been a smuggler just the way the whole lift played out, from stopping to driving away to all the boxes. To me, this person was a good driver regardless; they helped me when I needed help.

After a great sleep, I woke up and did my morning stretches, and I was back on the road. After a few kilometres, I decided to stop for water as the sun was beaming down hard, and I needed a refill.

From the border, I managed to cycle from Kastoria to Athens in three days. That's not too far under five hundred kilometres or three hundred miles—in three days. I was travelling at some speed and at some pace. There was not much time to write. There were several pages blank in the book. The highlight was Meteora and seeing a rotting Rottweiler along the road somewhere. There was not much else to see, but Meteora was out of this world. In Athens, I did see the Acropolis, which was something else—a magnificent structure. I actually saw a similar structure in Hampi, India. It looked very similar.

After leaving the city of Athens a few days later, about twenty kilometres out of the city, I began to feel something not quite right with the bicycle. The back wheel felt softer than usual. Great, a puncture. Off the highway I went. I saw a fruit stand and asked if there was any water, and I was directed to a hose. I filled a bucket with water and began to check the tube to see what was deflating the tyre. I found several thorns in the tyre. I spent my time fixing the tube as well as the spare tube. Some time passed, and the bicycle was rideable once again.

Back onto the highway, a few kilometres later, I came across a toll station. I asked the person at the counter if it was okay to pass; they then directed me somewhere to the right. I was not sure if they had asked me to get off the road or to stay on the right. I continued anyway. I saw a truck, and I asked the driver if I could have a lift, but the person was having trouble with the police. Best to head on down the road.

I continued to cycle; the back wheel was still giving me problems. I pulled to the side of the highway to a parking station, got the pump out, and began adding more air to the tube and tyre. It was still not completely inflated. I noticed a highway patrol vehicle passing on the other side of the road. I continued pumping and ignored. Two minutes later, I saw a police motorbike with the lights flashing, also on the other side. I thought it would be time to leave as this was the fourth time I was on the highway, and I didn't think I was allowed, though I was not certain. No, I was definitely not allowed on the motorway seeing as I was picked up on the way to Athens. I had been told to get off the motorway towards Athens; I was certain that I cannot cycle here.

I continued forwards, and a few kilometres later, I saw a McDonald's and decided to go in for some poor food and to take advantage of the free Wi-Fi. All I wanted to do was get my location to see about another route up north. Several minutes passed, and I saw a couple pull up in their van to the car park. I approached them and told them of the bicycle trouble that I was having. I asked if it would be possible to get a lift farther up the road. They went in for their food and returned with an employee to translate as there was a lack of understanding. The employee spoke very good english. They acted as translator between the Bulgarian couple and myself. A few minutes passed, and it was sorted.

We headed up the highway several hundred kilometres. As we continued up north, a heavy rain began to batter the van. *This is not good*, I thought. *Where am I going to sleep tonight?* I had my tent, but in the fierce rain, it'd be no good. I asked the Bulgarian people if it would be possible to sleep in the back of the van for the night. They didn't quite understand; as time progressed, it was time for all to go to sleep. I lay down in the back of the van, and I got out a towel and made a pillow to try to get some rest as, in the morning, I would be wondering where to go to next. There were many possibilities, but where to actually go?

At this stage, I felt lost in the town of Kavala. From Athens, I had travelled seven hundred kilometres north to an unknown place. I had not chosen this place, but the driver had. All the places I had been had been unknowns; this one was different though. It was much too far from where I was. It would have taken a week to get here, and that was what I had planned until the lift was available. It was not the easiest doing this without a smartphone but not impossible.

Time to compose myself, time to take deep breaths, time to get back on the saddle. I thanked the Bulgarian couple, and we parted ways. Off to an Internet cafe I went to look at Google Maps and to plan where I was going to next. At this stage, I was still very uncertain. Istanbul sounded like a place I should visit when I reached Turkey. Although after I headed through Turkey, this was as far as my Irish passport would get me visa-free. Did this mean I should stay in Europe?

I was still in the place of Kavala. I saw signs for the ferry and thought that I could maybe get away from the place. I asked a few of the boats where they were heading, mostly out into sea to catch fish and return. I'd pass on that. One boat gave me hope. One of the trawlers on the boat told me to get a jug of water and to wait. I could see the boat coming into the dock. Unfortunately, the boat was the same as the others and going out to sea to catch.

'Can I come anyway?' I said for a laugh.

'No', they replied.

At this stage, I was still not ready to vacate the vicinity, a shipping yard. I was too tired after the cycling and travelling to Athens and here. Or maybe it was the bicycle giving problems. It could have done with a service. I then went into the ferry terminal to see where the boats were heading, mostly to the island of Thasos. To Thasos I went. I decided to leave my bicycle at the ferry terminal as all I wanted to do on the island was sleep as I was completely drained of energy.

On the island, I found a secluded area free of people and out of view from passing cars. I had my tea and was able to get a few hours' sleep before taking a walk around the island. There was not much to be doing at nine o'clock at night. The restaurants and watering holes were open. I had my water though. I heard the next day there were boats at seven and ten o'clock in the morning.

I slept the night and had a powerful sleep, although my batteries were not fully charged as I was awoken by the sound of people walking outside the tent. I checked the time on the laptop, and it was six o'clock in the morning. I thought, *I'll get the next one.* I lay there to have a wee snooze, and then the person walking outside got to me. I decided to get up and pack up as soon as I could. I had camped in a shipping yard, and I was well aware that there would be activity in the morning, but I had not expected this. I leaped out of the tent, said hello, packed up, and ran/walked, kind of like a shuffle to the boat as I was not that enthusiastic. I missed the boat by five metres. I went to the beach beside the ferry port and set up camp while I waited for the next boat. Time passed, and I checked the time, five to ten. I quickly packed up my belongings and ran for the boat; luckily, there was still time. I headed for the ferry.

'You need a ticket,' the attendant said while pointing to a cabin.

I headed over and purchased a ticket, and I was back on the ferry and off to Kavala. The ferry was a reasonable size, with three floors and plenty of legroom and space to move about. In about an hour, the ferry arrived in Kavala.

During my time on the island, several things were on my mind, one of them was the bicycle. *What if someone steals a wheel? Pointless thinking. If it happens, it happens. No need to dwell on what could be. But this bicycle is like a car to me or even better. The only fuel I need is for myself. If the bicycle was stolen, it would not have been the end of the world. Life goes much further than material. But this bicycle is my transport.*

The ferry docked, and the bicycle was in sight. I headed towards the bicycle and unlocked it, and I was back on the saddle. Out of the port I went in search of a bicycle repair shop. I should have really left it in when I was on Thasos. I asked a younger person if they knew where there was a bicycle shop, and they took me there as there was one not far away. I left my bicycle in for the service. I explained to the person what the problem was, and they headed off on their moped. *Okay*, I thought. They went to pick up supplies to fix the bicycle.

There were two problems with the bicycle, one minor and one major. The minor problem was there was a switch which changed the compression in the front suspension from on-road to off-road. All that was needed was a cable to be reattached as, when I was in Croatia, I thought I was in a race while cycling the roads. Again, this was not reality; it was, however, madness. The other problem was the back wheel. I wanted new bearings as I thought that was my problem.

The person said to come back at two-thirty in the afternoon. I headed back at around three o'clock, and the place was closed with no one in sight. I could see my bicycle in the back of the shop, and I knew someone would be back in a matter of time. I sat opposite the shop and had lunch of bread, meat, and a yoghurt. Eventually, I saw someone entering the shop. I headed over. They didn't actually work there; they were only collecting a set of keys.

I saw my bicycle there and had a look; only the minor problem had been fixed but not the back wheel. This was still not spinning as many revolutions as the front. It was not free; therefore, there was a resistance. The person there explained that someone would be back in two or three hours.

I headed back to the cafe from the previous day to use the free Wi-Fi to plan a route out of Kavala and onto the next city, town, or village. I found a supermarket where I could pick up supplies for the journey later. I headed back to the bicycle shop, and—success—the person had returned. I explained and showed the person that the bicycle was still having problems. They said the bicycle was okay. I took my bicycle and brought it out the front. 'Are we good?' I said.

'That will be fifteen euros,' they told me.

'What for?' I laughed.

They had said that they had done something to the back wheel. 'No, you did not. It's still not working correctly,' I said.

'Okay, five euros', they replied.

I put my hand in my pocket and pulled out four euro ninety cents. 'Okay, that will do,' they replied.

With the bicycle now half fixed, I headed back on the road in search of Xanthi, a place closer to the Turkish border. I cycled about thirty kilometres and got a puncture at the side of the road. Thumb out, I tried to get a lift somewhere as it was dangerous at the side of the road. A person passed in their pickup truck; they drove past and then reversed. We put my bicycle in the back, and they drove a few kilometres to a restaurant where I could fix my bicycle.

A number of Greek people came over to help, but at the same time, they congregated around the bicycle. I got out the spare tube and replaced it. The people decided to get their own pump and whatnot as they could see the pump I was using was not as efficient. The three of them then tried to pump the tyre up while I began to fix my spare tube as I could hear a hiss from it. They continued trying to pump up the tyre with no luck. I then used mine and began to pump; slowly, the tyre began to inflate, and the wheel was now ready for more cycling. I had a jar of water with them, and told them my story and my plans.

'You are crazy,' one of them said. I put out my hand to say 'a little bit'. One of them did something similar to show 'very'. We all had a laugh. I thanked them again and shook hands with the owner of the restaurant, who was more than helpful, and I was back on the saddle.

I headed off down the road for Xanthi. I continued on the road, finally reaching three kilometres outside Xanthi. I had a choice to either continue on the road I was on or head into Xanthi. I chose to continue until I found a decent place to camp for the night. My bicycle was locked up at the service station across the road as I did not want to risk another puncture if I were to take it down the path to camp. I placed my camp as far away from the road as possible. I also had something to eat to cure the hunger before bed and then the usual pre-bed activities.

That morning, I awoke and disassembled my tent. I could see a large number of centipedes on the ground beneath; they must have been attracted to my body heat which radiated through the tent under layer, or it was a breeding ground. I could hear them moving while I was half asleep, the usual when you camp in the wild.

I had my breakfast and headed for Komotini. There was nothing really to see along the way apart from a large lake from the saddle, nothing really of interest, and I was in no mood to swim; plus, the weather was not great. At Potamia, I saw signs for natural thermal springs. I decided to follow the signs three kilometres off the road as I wanted to check it out and have a look and a bath.

When I arrived, it just looked like an abandoned estate with many derelict houses. I continued farther until I came to one of two buildings which seemed more in use than the others. A person came out and explained it would be four euros. I explained to them that I would only be there for five or ten minutes maximum. I headed on in for a quick dip and time for myself to reflect. I came to no real conclusion on what I was doing here apart from relaxing and having a wash. I got out of the thermal spring and dried myself, and I was back on the road.

I continued the cycle to Komotini. I found a Lidl and decided to pick up supplies for the rest of the day and farther down the road. I noticed the security guard was wearing a bulletproof or stab-proof vest, had a shaved head, and was a rather large person, a stereotypical bouncer working at the local supermarket.

I did my rounds, picking up what I needed. I was hungry and needed energy, so I picked up a bar of chocolate with the intention of paying and decided to start eating it. They then came running across to tell me that I cannot do this. I explained to them I was hungry and I was going to pay for the other half. They then followed me around the shop while I finished; unfortunately, they did not help me, just following. While they were concentrating on the foreigner, they could have been catching the real opportunists.

I left the store with my goods and headed off down the road. I arrived into the centre of Komotini and decided to ask someone if they knew where I could find a bicycle shop. Actually, I headed into a shop which had a load of bicycles out the front. I assumed it was a bicycle shop, and

I headed in, only to find out that it was a fishing shop. I found this random. I asked the person where I could find a bicycle shop, and they pointed to one down the road. I headed off. There, I explained the problem I was having. While here, I noticed there was a thorn in the back wheel, and I removed it, and the tyre obviously went flat.

I still thought it was the bearings that were giving me the problem with the back wheel. They told me that this was not the problem and rearranged the back disc brake, and successfully, the wheel was now freely moving without resistance. They asked if I would like a second-hand tyre for a fiver. I said yes, and the tyre was replaced. I got my spare tube and wheel fixed. I thanked the people for their good, cheap, and efficient work. Pity I found out later that the tyre company takes returns on their used products. They would certainly get more than a fiver for that tyre. Then again, there was no chance I would be carrying a tyre around with me. That would be too much; therefore, being able to trade and dispose of correctly was enough to console me.

I headed off into the centre to stop for a jug of water in one of the cafes. It was enjoyable. I got back on the saddle and headed to an unknown place along the road. On the road, I noticed large clouds forming in the distance; and still, I continued into the eye of the storm—bad move. The rain began at about four o'clock in the afternoon. I decided to set up camp in a forest I had seen from the road while it was still light. The rain profusely attacked the tent, and water was beginning to form puddles everywhere. I did what I could to keep the water out, but it kept on coming in… This is where a waterproof hammock would have come in handy… I purchased one in India…

The rain eventually died down. I packed up my tent and headed back on my bicycle. I got another flat tyre in the back. Now this was inevitable as, even though I took my time in fixing the tube at the Greek restaurant, I knew the tube was not fully fixed. I headed to a petrol station in the distance and asked if it was okay to fix my tube and said that I would need some water. I then took my time to ensure the tubes would be fixed properly and that I would be on the road as soon as I could. I really did take my time. Why should we be in a hurry? I was travelling. I had all the time in the world. Too many people are always in a rush.

The rain did not stop. In a matter of time, I made the decision to head off into the darkness. I put on my waterproofs, and on the saddle I went. It was dark, and the road was very wet; many cars were on the road at night. The rain was getting heavier, making it harder to see.

I came across an abandoned building where I could place my tent for the night but thought to myself I could get farther down the road, but in the end, I placed the tent under the comfort of a roof. There was a three-story building I used as my shelter, placing the tent on the second floor, free from the elements. The sleeping bag may have been slightly wet, but I did not let this deter me from getting a good sleep. This was what I would have to endure as I progressed farther east. I was ready for what lay in store. It would be a much more different type of travelling session seeing as I was now approaching mid-September. The weather was going to get progressively worse as I headed up north. There was nothing I can do about that, but I'd find shelter when I needed shelter.

In the morning, I packed up and was back on the bicycle. Everything felt good. The sun was hidden behind the clouds; the temperature and humidity were perfect for cycling. I took my time, eventually coming across a backpacking couple. As I was in no hurry, I decided to stop, and I was greeted by a friendly hello. We began to chat; they were a French couple who started off walking from Venice, Italy. They left around mid-June, about twenty days before I had left. *They have walked very fast,* I thought. Thus far, I have had about twenty days of rest in various cities and campsites, time where I could give my legs a rest from cycling—well, not really, more to relax as one of the great things about cycling is that you are sitting down. They ended up showing me a pouch of dirt they had been collecting from the various countries they had been in, and with this soil, they were adding soil from the new country to the pouch. Well that is one way to travel, far out too.

We shook hands and parted ways. I decided to stay at the shelter for a few more moments longer, rearranging my backpack before heading off down the national road. 'Au revoir, monsieur et madame!' I shouted from the bicycle as I zoomed past. I heard a response but wasn't quite sure of it, and I wasn't going to stop to find out.

Several kilometres down the line, I came across a large supermarket. I stopped in for a water bottle and a packet of biscuits to keep my energy levels up before I found greater food. I continued on the road, and I saw several signs for Alexandroúpoli. I continued along this road through the mountains and hills until I came across a sign for Via Egnatia, which had a silhouette of backpackers and of a Greek and chariot.

I decided this was the place I would have lunch. I continued on up the hill off the road until I reached an idyllic spot with a nice view over the valleys surrounded by the mountains. I thought half-heartedly, *Where are the chariots? Where is the racecourse?* I came to the conclusion that maybe back in the day this was where they raced; if not, those were very misleading signs. I finished off my lunch and was back on the road.

The hills had a small incline throughout. I progressed until I reached the top of the hill. Here, I was able to sit on the saddle all the way down the hill, enjoying freewheeling movement that I had earned after the energy used. I do enjoy those moments.

I saw a sign for Alexandroúpoli and continued. Along the way, I stopped off at a petrol station to refill my water bottle. I asked the attendant if the water was safe to drink. I shook the bottle of water, pointed to the tap, pretended to drink, and threw a thumbs up and a down. The assistant replied with a thumbs up. Good enough for me. I then continued on the road with Alexandroúpoli in sight. I came across a Lidl along the way, and I headed inside to pick up my lunch, enough calories to do me until the morning.

Throughout the day, the front wheel had been giving me small problems as it was not fully inflated. I stopped at one petrol station to see about a pump—no luck, only a car pump. They explained to me that it would be hard to find what I needed as it was a Saturday afternoon. I headed forwards in search of the next petrol station. Here, I asked and showed my valve, a Presta valve. They then came back in a moment with attachments for the pump. Within a matter of time, the tyre was fully pumped.

On the bicycle I went into the centre of Alexandroúpoli. I came across a tourist centre and headed over. It turned out it was more of a campsite with information about the campsite. Anyway, I found out the information I needed, only another forty-five kilometres to the Turkish border. The centre was busy enough for a Saturday afternoon. I found a cafe, and I was able to use the Wi-Fi to find out exactly where I was and the exact distance to Turkey. Even though I had a paper map throughout, I felt more comfortable with a digital representation. Off I went on some very long roads past the airport on my way to the border.

At this time, the sun was going down, and clouds were beginning to form. I had to make a decision—continue into the eye of the storm or take a break where there was clear blue sky and the sun was going down. Now this was not an easy decision to make. I had taken my time in doing so and was somewhat rewarded.

Someone came out from a garage opposite to where I was contemplating, who was also travelling and taking shelter. They invited me into the safe and secured area that happened to be a mechanic shop. At the time of the night, I was unsure of what lay ahead in Turkey; it could have been dangerous around the border. I was thankful for the offer. At first, I was reluctant to stay as I wanted to cross the border that night. They asked why. I only had the one answer; I wanted to.

That night, I camped outside the garage. It was safe, and I knew everything would be good in the morning. That morning I awoke, packed up my tent, had a jug of water, and made the decision to stay another day if possible as I was not fully prepared to leave the abode. Previously, I had planned several days of rest as I had been on the trot for many days. I would cross the border when the time was right.

That night, I did not have the best of sleep. Instead of setting the tent up outside like the previous night, I set it up inside the garage, but I had not anticipated how much warmer it would be compared with the outside that I had become accustomed to. But when I went outside for fresh air and to cool down, I went back, and the remainder of the sleep was a good one. The sound person had given me a foam mat to lie on. I had been lying on the solid ground since I began, which was no problem to me, less to carry. I concluded that it was still the heat and not the mat; if anything, the mat should have made it more comfortable.

Now apparently, you needed to be crossing the Turkish border in a vehicle; they did not accept pedestrians. The person I was with was walking to Jerusalem or somewhere religious. For some reason, I left the garage after they did, enjoying a nice cup of Nescafé while I was there. I didn't think about this until I was on the road. I really should have left first. I never thought about the road conditions until I was on the road, and it would have been better if I was aware. I digressed; it shouldn't make a difference as I would have to continue forwards to reach my next destination. There was no going back; that would be tedious to return the way I came. I wouldn't be doing that unless it was necessary.

It was fifteen kilometres to go to reach the border. I reckoned it would have taken me less than an hour, but I never took into consideration the wind that was battering me, opposing my motion, and nearly pushing me off the road. This took me longer than I expected. I could see the border patrol, and I pushed onwards and crossed through the first checkpoint without hesitation or bother. I then crossed the river Maritsa that separates Greece from Turkey. I gave several thumbs up to the army who were patrolling; several acknowledgements I received.

I then saw the person from the mechanic shop. At one point, I saw another person with a big beard. I took my hands off the handlebars, threw them in the air, and shouted, 'Freedom!' They laughed, and so did I. Even I didn't know what I meant. It was a bit of craic though.

I met the person from the mechanic shop, and we went to the next patrol; they went first. There were problems with their passport as it had been through the wash recently. I got through fine using the Irish passport, paying twenty-five euros for a ninety-day visa. Before, when the person was in duty-free, two people approached them and asked questions about their passport, their whereabouts, and other personal questions. This made them weary of the whole situation when they were trying to get through. The same two people talked to the police people working at the border patrol. Shady business.

The person I was with made the decision to head back to the car garage and cross tomorrow or later that evening. They asked what I would do. I said I would find a place in the shade on the grass to relax for a moment before I made a decision. A short time passed, and we headed off in separate directions. They returned to Greece; I continued into Turkey.

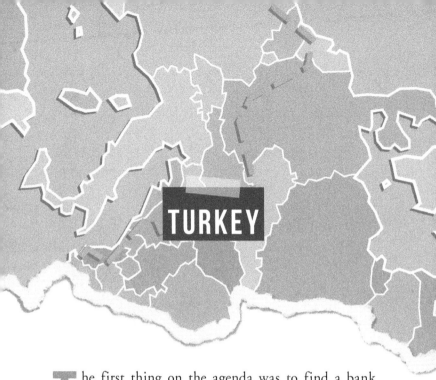

TURKEY

The first thing on the agenda was to find a bank to change euro into Turkish lira. When I arrived, it was one o'clock in the afternoon. All the banks were closed at half past twelve for an hour, which I found strange. I guessed it was for lunch. I ventured around the small town of İpsala on the bicycle where I scoped out the place—supermarkets, banks, and library. In no time, it was half past one, and I headed off to the bank, only to be redirected by the security guard to a post office around the corner. I followed their directions. I did come across several banks along the way, but I listened to the guard. I wanted to change money, and people always recommend a post office.

I arrived there and waited in line for a good twenty minutes before being served. A few Turkish people did skip the queue. I was in no hurry; therefore, I was not offended. I gave over fifteen euros to receive forty-two Turkish lira. I had heard previously that the exchange rate was two and a half per euro. I was happy to receive what I did.

From here, I needed water. I availed to a cafe in the centre and used their services such as Wi-Fi and power.

Here, I was able to respond and send emails as well as apply for visas online for other foreign countries that needed a visa before arrival such as Iran. I also delved into the digital realm to update a blog which I had set up the previous week in Kavala. I drank several jugs of water, and it was time to leave. I exchanged words and acknowledgement with one of the workers and then left the cafe.

As I was leaving, 'Monsieur, monsieur', called the cafe attendant. I knew what they were calling me about, payment for the jug of water. I thought we had agreed that I would just be getting it free of charge for no reason. We had not agreed. When I had asked for the bill, there must have been a misunderstanding as there was no response. I threw my thumb up to suggest a yes, and they responded appropriately. They did not show me the bill; therefore, I walked out but happily returned to pay in front of all the customers. Entertainment for them.

Now it was time for lunch. I collected my supplies. I wasn't sure of the best meat. I headed to several places before I made a purchase. I had enough to do me for a few days. I then headed out of the village of İpsala to find a place to eat in the shade free of people. I chose the corner of a field, sat on a rounded bale, and ate my food.

When I had finished, I relaxed. I heard gunshots every so often. I assumed they were hunters, but no bullets had come my way as I occasionally looked to see where they came from. It did sound as if the person was changing directions. It would be best to leave soon.

In the end, I decided to go over and investigate as I saw a person looking at the crops. I left the area in the corner of the field and headed towards the sound of fire. I approached the shed where there was a farmer, and I saw a device that looked like a mortar. The device was firing, though nothing was being launched. I had a closer look, and it was a pneumatic device used to fire air from a shaft. I now understood the device was used to scare away birds and other animals from the crops. I concluded that, in Turkey, this was what they used instead of the common scarecrow, which was widely used across the world. Quite smart, though it sounded like a waste of energy.

I left the area and headed towards the centre once more. I made a decision to head back across the border to Greece. It was only twenty kilometres away. Why was I going back? There were several reasons. One was that I had left a jersey that belonged to a person from Scotland and it didn't even belong to them. I wanted to be able to give that back when I returned as this jersey had served me well through the twelve countries that I had cycled through. I was close to turning back around towards Turkey but decided I would continue as I was nearly there. I arrived to the garage, hopped over the fence, and looked to see if there was any sign of the jersey. I got it and headed back on the road towards Turkey.

That night, I cycled several kilometres over the border to İpsala. It was late, and I wasn't going to cycle anymore that night as I did not know what lay ahead in the darkness. I came across a building with the lights on beside a grassy area. I called in and asked if I could place a tent for the night. A phone call later, and yes, I could. I was shown to a place where I could camp. Now when I placed my tent, it was dark, and all I wanted to do was lie down and give my legs a rest. This night was no different, although the tent was placed ten metres from the road that led into the centre of the town. Cars had passed every so often; sleep was had, albeit not in one go, but it was had.

In the morning, I took my time, got up, and ready for the day. With the tent disassembled and the backpack ready to go, I walked towards the bicycle, and I noticed it had a flat tyre at the back. It looked like I would have

, anto type seg

to fix this before I was to go anywhere. I was able to bring it around to the building, which turned out to be an auto station. There was a bath of water, so it was a smooth operation fixing the tube. I thanked those who were around to help me, and on the road to Kesan I went.

There was nothing eventful on the road to Kesan, up and down hills on the highway/national road. Compared with the Albanian hills, this was much easier as it was constant and consistent unlike the Albanian hills, which were forever changing. When I arrived to Kesan, I noticed a Burger King and called in for Wi-Fi but had no luck. I was directed to a cafe by a security guard. When I arrived at the shopping park, there was a young child with a tin in their hand with snacks, who also noticed me and wanted me to buy something.

I did. All I had was fifty cents; they were happy for the money.

As I was walking to the cafe, the young child was following me. I finished my wander and found the cafe. The security guard wouldn't let them in. I had a jug of water and used the facilities, and I was back to my bicycle I had locked up outside Burger King. Luckily, both wheels were still attached.

When there, a Turkish person had asked where I had come from and where I was going. I answered accordingly. They had also asked about my studies and if I was an engineer. Before leaving, they gave me some glasses of water. 'Thank you, sir,' I said.

They then walked away, and as they entered Burger King, they signalled over to see if I was hungry. I responded appropriately, and the person bought me a Whopper meal and introduced me to their child. They left, and I enjoyed my meal peacefully.

By the time I had finished the meal, it was well after midday, and I did not want to be cycling in that heat. I found an area outside which had umbrellas that provided shade. I sat there and enjoyed my own company before I headed down the road towards my next stop.

There was a lot of construction on the roads. Many people were out on the roads doing their jobs. I continued up and down the hills. I could see that the road stretched quite a distance. I had cycled a considerable distance and decided I would have a rest in a forest parallel.

When I arrived, I could see smoke coming from the bushes. It was going to be either a forest fire or people. I decided to go over and investigate the area. When I approached the smoke, I could see a family sitting down to their lunch. I had gone too far and thought that it would be very strange if I turned away. I decided to head over and introduce myself. They invited me to sit down and have lunch with them. I agreed, and I enjoyed some very nice Turkish cuisine. There was a language barrier, but that was something that I was used to. Every time I finished a piece of food,

I was offered another. I wasn't too sure if they were on holiday or if they were a travelling Turkish family. I wasn't sure if the meat I was eating was bought or hunted or for human consumption. I ate and enjoyed anyway, same with the vegetables. I decided to ask a few questions, which was probably not the smartest idea considering the language barrier. When I did ask, it was just pure awkwardness.

In the background, there was Turkish music playing. This was the first authentic music I had heard on my travels, and I enjoyed it. The family could see this and acknowledged this. My head was banging ever so slightly. Lunch was nearly over, and the grandmother of the family made me a sandwich for the road. We continued to eat. I enjoyed the family atmosphere, and the food was delicious. From their van, one of the children put on music, everyone was on their feet dancing, and I joined in. It felt like I was drunk with joy, or maybe I had eaten too many foreign mushrooms. I enjoyed the experience.

It was time to go. I shook several hands. They fed me well, and I didn't want to be rude and decline; therefore, I continued to eat. By the end of it, I was stuffed and had plenty left over for later that evening. I thanked them for their hospitality, and away I went.

I was on the road for another few kilometres before I had to rest. I called into a house at the side of the road where there was a helicopter at the side.

There was a person sitting out the front. I asked if I could have some water. They showed me to a water cooler. I drank and drank, and my belly was fuller. I needed a rest, so I sat with them and told them a story. They were from Ukraine, they were in Turkey the last two months. I could have connected a few dots but decided it'd be best not to question. I thanked them for their hospitality, and off I went.

I climbed and climbed the hill until I reached the top. My belly was still sore. I saw a lorry driver outside their cabin. I asked for a lift, which they were happy to do. My bicycle was attached to the lorry, and down the hill we went. While sitting in the cabin, I could see that I would have been rewarded with several kilometres of downhill riding. I enjoyed the view from the cabin, smooth riding.

Eventually, the lorry went into the ferry station and was loaded onto a ferry. I stayed put as I did not want to leave the comfort of the cabin. The ferry was crossing the peninsula. Out of the truck we went and proceeded to the ferry deck.

The driver asked if I wanted tea, and tea was had. Time passed. I asked if they wanted a Fanta. I got a thumbs up. I headed into the cafe and asked for two Fantas. The cost was six Turkish lira. I put my hand into my pocket and pulled out five Turkish lira. That was enough. They must have known I was travelling and probably thought I had little to no money seeing as I probably looked scruffy and was wearing a Croatian jersey.

The ferry was ready to dock. The driver and I parted ways. They were heading left towards Kepez. I was heading right towards Çanakkale.

It was early, so I decided to find a cafe to use Wi-Fi. I waited around for service, eventually getting fed up, and headed into the back of the cafe to make myself a jug of water.

By this time, I had turned my Croatian jersey inside out to not disrespect the locals. After I had made my coffee, the attendant came in. I sort of apologised; they said it was cool and not to worry. I wasn't going to.

I found the road to Çanakkale and proceeded towards it. It was getting dark, and I cycled as far as I could before taking a break for the night as I had planned to reach the place by morning. I found a field with a great view over the peninsula and set up camp. I ate some food and had a look at the orange moon and stars. I looked up and saw the constellation that looked like the Big Dipper.

I assumed it was; I wasn't going to argue with myself.

When I ate and prepared the tent, I could hear several animals making noises. I wondered what was making the rustling sound. I grabbed the torch and went over to investigate. It was a wee hedgehog. I could see its wee little face; it looked scared. I turned off the light, and away it went. It was time for bed.

That morning, I awoke, took my time getting ready, and put away my tent. I had a spot of breakfast, and I was on the road again. It was only another forty kilometres to Çanakkale along the Turkish highway, which was not flat, it continually went up and down, engineers never think of the people who cycle, though it is not really their problem to solve. Maybe in the future this is something to solve when we turn away from fossil fuels and start relying on the abundant green energy.

I passed several fruit stands. I waved to one from the other side of the road, and a person smiled and waved back.

I cycled a few metres more and decided to cross the road to pick up some fruit for the day. They offered me a seat. I sat there and enjoyed an apricot and an apple before I headed towards the city, only another twenty kilometres.

I continued along the highway, with the same view repeating, very boring. I eventually reached the city border and could see activity in the distance. I headed along the road towards the outskirts. I began to question my route towards İzmir. Why was I heading there? There were not many consulates or embassies for countries that I was thinking about, just a city beside the sea. I headed towards the centre, following signs for the ferryboat. Eventually, I reached the destination to find out there was no ferry to Istanbul, even though the signs directed me there. The ferry was going back across the peninsula. No good.

I called into the tourist office to get a map of Turkey and to find out information on İzmir. I headed into the centre square, had lunch, and refilled up on water from a fountain for the road ahead. *Time to go*, I thought. I was off back down the same road in the midday heat. It was uncomfortable.

Eventually, I came across a large supermarket and shopping centre, Kipa Extra, like a Turkish Tesco. I picked up supplies and snacked some more. I left, and on the road to İzmir I went. The heat was really getting to me. I stopped off at a bus stop and lay down on the bench.

I decided to ask someone if I should head to İzmir, a really stupid question as I was the only one who can answer that. There would be no convincing otherwise. They didn't speak much english. I used my standard hand signals, thumbs up for İzmir. A car approached, the person put out their fingers, and the car stopped. People got out, and I asked them the same question. They were able to show me where İzmir was on the map and all the other places I should visit along the way. I thanked the couple, and away they went. 'Good luck!' they shouted from the car.

I began to really contemplate my travels to İzmir. It was very out of the way. I decided to make a sign for İzmir to see if someone could give me a lift.

At the time, I did not want to use my energy to get to the unknown place of İzmir. Time passed quite a bit, several hundred cars also probably passed, and one motorcycle passenger put up their middle finger as I stood at the side of the road with a sign against my backpack. The midday heat was decreasing. I contemplated heading back up north towards Istanbul and forgetting about İzmir. 'Five more lorries', I said to myself in the hope one of the five was successful.

There was a large stream of traffic, a few lorries drove past, and each declined the lift. The next two were up. The two lorries drove past at the exact same time; only one was able to decline the lift. I decided that I would wait for one more lorry. Success! A lift to İzmir was arranged. I loaded my bicycle and backpack into the back of the truck. And off to İzmir we went.

Now this was a very strange lift. This person was friendly. You know, the person had somewhat of a travelling companion, the hitchhiker. This person gave me a lift, and if some altercation arose, I would be prepared. The person asked if I wanted to drive the lorry. I was kind of like, *Okay*. Then they pointed to their lap. I declined their offer. Weird. This wasn't awkward at all. Was this a sign of things to come in Turkey?

I continued to enjoy my free lift to İzmir. It would have taken me days to cycle. The person was on and off the phone; I was slightly suspicious. They handed me the phone to speak to someone who could speak english. I had a conversation with the person about nothing really. I didn't really understand what they were saying, but I was able to tell them where I was from and where I had come from. The message was translated. Like the good human I am, I offered the driver some of the food I had.

Later on, it was time for a stop. We stopped at the side of the road, they headed out of the lorry, and I stayed put. Several minutes later, they called me, and I headed out. They were with a friend who was super. They asked if I wanted tea. I was like, *"Yeah, sure."* We headed down a lane, unsure where I was going, and we headed into a house. It was the parent's house of the second person—safe.

They fed me, we chatted, we laughed, I talked and someone translated, and they were fascinated. I was fed again with more tea, bread, cheese, tomatoes, and biscuits—a little feast. The Turkish people really were friendly and highly hospitable. When it was time to go, the person of the house packed up some biscuits and cake for the road ahead. One of the people arranged with the driver that I would be getting a lift back to Istanbul. We shook on it. I thanked everyone there for their hospitality, and back in the truck we went.

I saw signs for İzmir, and the distance was decreasing. Eventually, we arrived to İzmir. This was one massive city. The driver kept on driving until we reached a truck stop. I got my backpack and washed up. I decided to set up camp in the back of the person's lorry.

It was kind of what I had planned to do. I did not even want to close my eyes in the lorry with the driver.

That night, I had a cracker sleep, one of the best I had all week, as while cycling the roads, there were not many places to sleep with complete silence as the main road was near, unless you went very far out of the way, but that was not for me—well, not every night. When I was cycling and travelling many kilometres per day, I just wanted to sleep and didn't necessarily care where, as long as it was safe. That was the main priority.

In the morning, I saw the driver, and they wanted me out of their trailer. Fair enough. Mission complete. Time to explore İzmir at eight o'clock in the morning. The first attraction that I came across was the Atatürk Stadium. I cycled the perimeter, found an open door, and headed in. It was the athletes' warm-up room. I used the toilet and finished up. I found a young athlete and signalled for the showers. They pointed to the adjacent room—handy. I headed in for my shower, rearranged my backpack, and took my time to get ready for the day ahead. I even had time and the facility to charge my laptop. I did not shave that day. I would wait for another opportunity to do that. I finished up. I was able to lighten the load in my backpack by throwing away items that were once a necessity.

I headed back into the warm-up area and asked two athletes if I can get into the stadium arena. They did not really understand. One kind of pointed and then opened up Google Translate. They were unsure. They asked their coach, who pointed me out of the building. I quickly did a few laps of the area, and out the door I went.

I came across an entrance with two workers who said I could not enter and pointed on around the building. Success. I found an area with no workers present and proceeded up the stairs. I could feel a draught coming from somewhere; around the corner, I found another stairwell that led to the arena. I headed up the stairs, and the stadium was completely empty.

I hopped on the bicycle and did a quick half lap to the middle of the stadium as I wanted a photograph. I had charge in the laptop for a webcam photograph. I included the bicycle as it had been the force behind my accomplishment. Well, no, I had been the force through food and energy, and the bicycle was the mechanical wonder. Without the bicycle, I would be somewhere else in Europe, though I had always planned—well, not actually planned but utilised the mechanical greatness of the bicycle. And I have to an extent. A lift here and there, and I am down with that. It was more the fact that people were willing to give you a lift; they were random and usually asked for when necessary.

Time to head out and into the centre of İzmir to scope the place out as this was a new city, and I didn't know how long I would be here. I was cycling on a busy road with the morning traffic; I enjoyed this. It kept me alert as there were cars pulling out, parking, and stopping as well as pedestrians. City cycling was great fun for a wee while. I felt I was getting closer but also farther from the centre. I was using the two Folkart Towers as a marker as I knew they were near the centre.

A few kilometres later, I approached an area where I could see the sea. I followed the road through to the centre. This place was huge. I continued along the road until I came to the promenade. I got off the bicycle for a rest as I looked at the areas across the water, the seafront.

I asked a walker a simple question. Or maybe it was not so simple considering there was a language barrier. I asked them if the land opposite was all İzmir; they didn't understand. They took out their phone and called their friend who could speak english. 'I was asking your friend if the stretch of land in front was İzmir,' I said to the person on the phone. It was a different area. I was advised to take a boat there. İzmir first, and if I decided to head over there, I would use my trusted bicycle.

One of the first tasks I had to do was change money. I went to a bank and another, eventually being redirected to a different bank. I headed in and asked to change money, and I was pointed to an automated money changer. With money changed, now I needed to find somewhere to sit and enjoy the new surroundings which I had found.

Off I went to a cafe. I sat, I planned, and I drank jugs of water. One fact I found out was that Turkey abolished the death penalty several years ago—extreme. Then again, there are certain countries which still practice capital punishment. Nothing to worry about. At least they had abolished it.

I ventured around some more, and I found a place in the shade for lunch. I came across a large park in the centre of the city, Kultur Park. This would be my area away from the centre. I did a lap of the park and befriended a little kitten while I was having my lunch. I gave it some food. No bread for this cat, only meat. Another cat came over, and then there was a troop of cats in front of me. I stroked each of them and fed them. I noticed most of the cats had cuts and scratches, which was understandable. The park was a like a cat hive. No wonder they came here with the amount of people, plenty of food to be dispersed and plenty of scraps to be had after the visitors were done feeding, plus the attention.

I said my goodbyes to each of them, and I was back on the saddle. I headed towards a supermarket to pick up supplies for the day ahead. It was going to be a good day. I headed back to the park and set up an eating area. My sleeping bag was out; it was time to sit back, relax, and enjoy the sun and food, all with a bottle of water.

Two young hooligans came over and took my spot, casually sitting on my sleeping bag. They asked if I wanted a jar of water. They asked me three times, and on the third occasion, I had a jar with them. I asked if they were hungry. One put their hand in my backpack and grabbed out some bananas for the both of them.

Fair enough.

Things began to get heated. Out of nowhere, the young person pushed me. I stood strong. It got more confrontational. They started yelling and getting on, causing a scene. The police came over in a matter of minutes. They went towards a tree and broke a branch, not heavy enough to throw. They found a rock and threw it towards me. Not much power, but they tried. I volleyed the rock as it was coming in my direction. The confrontation was over. The police signalled, *Okay?*

"Yes, nothing to see here," I said as the situation had diffused.

I finished my lunch and decided to have a snooze. I was awoken by the sound of people shouting in the distance. I immediately thought of football. I took my time rising from my slumber, and on the bicycle I went towards the noise. It was a demonstration/protest. I saw about fifty riot squad members standing at the side of the road.

They were not really paying attention but waiting. I headed off down the road; it was a very peaceful protest. Nothing to see there.

I eventually came across an area which was heavily populated with people and with shops selling clothing, actually many different shops. I came across a street; Shoe Street I would call it. It was a shoe bazaar. One made a connection. I responded as I was in need of a new pair of shoes to replace the old ones which had become too worn.

Leather sandals would be the best bet. I was shown several pairs, all very nice. They showed me a pair, maybe about fifty Turkish lira.

'I need a pair to replace these. The lower cost, the better,' I said to the shoe keeper.

They showed me a pair for fifteen Turkish lira. 'They will do,' I said. I tried them out on the bicycle first before I made the purchase. They worked, no slipping.

I was asked if I would like a jug of water. 'Sure,' I replied. A few minutes later, a jug of Turkish water arrived with two pieces of Turkish delight. It was my first Turkish jug, and it was delicious. Money was exchanged for the sandals. I was offered water, and I accepted. Hands were shook, and off down the shoe bazaar I went.

I reached the end of the bazaar, and I heard a friendly voice say something in an American-english accent. 'Yo, man, where are you from?' they said. I responded accordingly. From there, I was offered more jugs of water. They invited me into their shop; we had a chat and then ran some errands. We arranged to meet up another night. They were able to direct me to a campsite about twenty kilometres down the promenade. I set off on my bicycle and somehow ended up back at the bazaar; they set me on the right path and towards a campsite for the night.

This was the first real cycling I had done in a few days. Along the promenade, there was wind fighting against me the whole way. I continued and eventually stopped at a restaurant for a break. I found a grassy area out the back free from people with a single table. I put my supplies on the table, prepared my food, and began to munch.

Four people approached the table, four burly people. I assumed they were the owner and friends. I was right, and they were not happy with how I was sitting at their table. They told me it was a dangerous area and that I was to leave. I finished eating my food, taking my time, of course, and on my bicycle I went towards the campsite.

The stretch of road was heavily populated with watering holes, clubs, and apartments. *Where am I going to camp?* I asked two pedestrians if they knew where I could camp. They directed me towards a hill with a square box that went up and down. 'A tram?' I said to the person.

'Yes, a tram. I will not forget that,' they said. What I really meant to say was cable car. I thanked them, and away I went. (I have since corrected myself.)

A few minutes passed, and I heard someone calling. It was the two people. I was invited to stay for the night. *Great*, I thought. They bought Turkish food from a deli. When we arrived at the house, the food was demolished. Time passed, and it was getting late. I was asked a few times if I was tired or wanted sleep. I didn't know if I was being rude. I assumed so as it was not my home, and I continued to stay up and enjoy their company in a warm atmosphere. Plus, there was water on tap.

Eventually, I went to bed and had a great sleep, although I did wake up with three new bite marks. What has bitten me? I didn't know. I was sure it was nothing too serious. Maybe one of the cats; it was a possibility. I got out of bed and headed in to see the others. All was well.

Now the first thing I should have done was to have asked about the whereabouts of a supermarket to pick up breakfast for us all. I was distracted, and food was not really on my mind. It was when I first awoke but not when I had arose from the bed.

It was approaching the early afternoon, and the owner put on a fairly intense and emotional short film called *Six Shooter* starring Brendan Gleeson. For half an hour, we sat in silence, watching. It was powerful. I must have seen this before; it looked, sounded, and felt like something I had previously watched. It was good.

I went to my backpack and got out biscuits for the people. I was offered biscuits, and then a Turkish sandwich came along. All was enjoyed.

I began to think about leaving. I headed for a shower and got ready for the day ahead. We shook hands, and I got ready to depart. I was told to hold on a second, and the owner returned with a bag, a pen, and a notepad. 'This will come in handy,' I said happily. I had been holding out on a bag, to be honest, as I knew somewhere down the line I would come across one, not necessarily from a person, but I would find one. And well, I did. This would be handy for when I visited another city, and I was able to carry around what I needed and leave what I didn't somewhere else. I thanked the two for their hospitality and friendliness, and away I went.

As I was cycling, I turned around to throw the hand up for the final wave, and I almost crashed, slamming on the front hydraulic disc brake and being projected forwards. I calmly collected myself. And on the road towards İzmir, along the promenade I went.

I cycled passed two people on the promenade who were enjoying the sunshine. I stopped, chatted with them, and introduced myself. They were Russians, very nice but also crazy. I jest, of course. They offered me jars of water, but I was reluctant to drink but accepted and drank with them. They mentioned something about a haircut. I said I would find a cheap haircut in the centre. One of the Russians opened their purse, took out twenty Turkish lira, and forced it into my pocket.

Again, I was reluctant, but they were adamant. We continued to drink. Two Turkish people had been watching and preying on the two Russians like vultures. Time approached, and time passed. I finished my drink and thanked the people, and away I went in search of a haircut.

I went to several places, which were probably salons. All I needed was a haircut. I finally settled on a place that would cut for twelve Turkish lira, about three pound sterling. My hair was cut and washed with change left over for my tea. I found a cafe close to the Kultur Park and enjoyed the ambient environment for a few hours before finding a place to camp that night.

That morning, I awakened, took my time getting ready, and headed to the Kultur Park for a relaxed afternoon as, that night, I was heading back to the bazaar to meet the person from the shop for a night out in İzmir.

When I arrived, hands were shook. 'You want tea?' they asked as I arrived. They picked up a phone to order; several minutes later, I have a tea in my hand. I then headed off to find somewhere to get changed for a Saturday evening in İzmir. I changed from my cycling attire in a restaurant.

Four of us headed out into the town. First stop was a restaurant for some traditional food and several glasses of a traditional Turkish liquor, raki, and several glasses of water. Next stop was a watering hole on the seafront which was populated with people. Then it was a night of drinking jars of water and small craic. We headed up for a large pitcher of water, and we drank several. Next stop was a nightclub. A few hours had passed, and for an unknown reason, we were asked to leave out of nowhere—well, not exactly. There was a small confrontation.

Anyway, we left the club in search of the next place to go. That would be a hotel, twenty pound sterling for the night for a ten-hour sleep, an expense that I had never accounted for. Pity I left my belongings in the back of the shop along with my bicycle, or I would have been camping somewhere in the city. It had to be done. I had nowhere else to sleep that night and was happy to shed the twenty. When I arrived to the room, I had a flask of water and put on a wildlife programme about lions and drifted off to sleep. In the morning, I awakened, headed down for a glass of water, and relaxed in the non-existent atmosphere. 'Time to check out,' said a person.

The previous night, it had been arranged that I would have the room for twenty-four hours; then all of a sudden, the arrangement had been made void. I knew this was not how a hotel worked, but if the employee or manager says you can have the room until later on in the day, you should get the chance; but yes, this was rarely the case unless they were really sound, and the place was not too busy. Anyway, I waited and pondered, eventually handing my key into reception. They were glad to get rid of me.

When I left the hotel, I headed back to the centre, picking up a litre bottle of natural cherry juice as part of my breakfast, natural goodness which was probably processed. Then I came across a doner kebab stand and had one of those as well, only because the person asked, 'Are you hungry?' And well, I was. The next stop was to go to the bazaar to change my clothing and collect several items that I would need that day before heading back at night to collect.

That afternoon was another relaxed one with plenty of food and water, a casual Sunday. A number of shops were closed, though most were open to continue their trade to get that cash money from the visiting people—cash money as these shops did not really operate with chip and pin. The department stores accepted chip and pin but mostly in the bazaars it was cash.

I returned later on that evening to the bazaar, and luckily, it was still open. I headed upstairs to grab my backpack and off in search of a place to camp that evening. I knew that night I would be camping at the Atatürk Stadium. When I was first at the stadium, I noticed there were several people camping. My first thought was that it was noble athletes who had nowhere else to go and were camping outside their place of refuge. I knew where I was camping, but I wasn't quite sure how I would be getting there apart from cycling. The roads that I would be cycling were all highways. The road that I had cycled to the centre from the stadium was not as much highway. I asked a few people along the highway, who were able to direct me there.

When I arrived to the stadium, there was a function happening at a restaurant saloon; it shouldn't give me too much bother as I had slept through worse, and I was tired. I asked the campers if I can camp there. They basically told me to clear off. I found the security office, which I had passed upon entry. I asked the security guard if it was okay to camp. They were more than helpful, and they said that it was okay. There was a saloon that was playing music until ten o'clock. Luckily, I fell asleep before that.

I was awakened by the sun beaming through my tent and also by the sound of several work people working around my tent. I let them work and continued to rest until I was ready to rise. I saw some insects walking about the tent floor, and I quickly removed them. It was time to get up.

I headed to the bathroom of the saloon, but it was closed. I returned to the athlete's warm-up room, where I was able to use the facilities. I forgot my towel. A shower would have to wait until later.

Before leaving the tent, I packed a lunch as I had the plan of heading into the arena to sit in the shade. The place was completely empty. I found a seat made of plastic, but it was too hot to sit on. I looked over to the centre of the arena, and there was a patch of leather seats. That would do me rightly, and away I went to have a comfortable seat in the shade. I sat there for about an hour or two eating lunch, relaxing, and writing. I found that, in the city, it is much harder to attain peace and quiet. I preferred quieter areas free from people, and the stadium offered this.

I finished up and headed back to the tent. I had no worries about leaving my backpack there as I had all my valuables with me. It was time for a wash. I quickly packed away my tent, and off into the centre I returned.

I decided to head to the Kultur Park as there was a masjid, a place for Muslims to pray and practice Islam. This place was like a sanctuary. I had been using it throughout my stay in İzmir as it was a very quiet and peaceful place away from the city, though still within a reasonable distance of the conveniences. I headed there to relax and to meditate/sleep. I got comfortable. Throughout my travels, this had been one of the most comfortable places to rest, mainly due to the carpet which I used to lie down on. You don't often get that in the wild. I am not a Muslim for the record. I used this place as a safe haven away from the crowded streets. It was time to go.

Off I went to see the person from the retail store. I headed through the busy streets on the bicycle, speeding through when I got the chance and then slamming on the front hydraulic disc brakes when a person walked without looking. The streets were covered with illuminated signs and stalls selling various goods. I arrived to the bazaar. 'You want tea?' someone asked.

'Yes, please', I replied. I drank my tea and then headed around to the store.

Their guardian said they had gone home with a toothache or another lame excuse. *Something is not quite right*, I thought. It was Sunday night for the record. Their guardian told me about a container or a ferry or a vessel coming into the harbour on Monday morning. They explained that the ferry entered the port once a week, a cruise ship. At the time, I didn't know what they were angling at. I wasn't sure if I was to deliver a shipment or bring in customers to the shop. A delivery I would do. They asked me to come in at nine thirty in the morning.

'I will see what I can do,' I replied.

That night, I ate a lot of food, a mixture of good and bad, healthy and unhealthy snack foods. I just wanted a quick source of energy. I was walking the streets of İzmir. It would have been about eight o'clock in the evening. I came across a new area that I had never walked before, a busy market street with much activity for yet another day. I stopped off in the middle of the square and sat down at a table. Next thing I knew, I was drinking a cup of tea—excellent.

As I sat there alone, a person came over, sat down, and asked if I would like a flask of water. They were from Syria, living in Turkey. I tried not to ask too many questions but could understand why they had fled their country and found another life elsewhere. They were using their phone, and I noticed the wallpaper—three Syrian fighters each kitted out with guns, protective gear, and camouflage. They pointed to one. 'My brother', they said. I wasn't shocked; they were from Syria after all. They may have been having a laugh, but I took it as the truth. Syria was not a place I would want to visit on my bicycle.

I finished my tea and shook hands, and away down the markets I walked. I saw several *otels* along the way. I called into the first one. 'You have a room?' I said.

'Where you from?' asked the person.

'Ireland', I replied.

'Ten lira,' they said.

Now at the time I did not even have ten Turkish lira on me. I said that I would be back in ten minutes. I didn't even leave my backpack at the *otel*. I just left as I was unsure whether I wanted to stay in a hotel or camp. I found a Wi-Fi hotspot to respond to emails while I pondered. Did I want to stay indoors or camp? It was less than a few pound sterling to stay at the *otel*. Eventually, I headed back to the *otel* to find the room was not available. I really should have left my backpack there to show genuine interest. But I was unsure if I wanted to camp. Where would I sleep tonight?

I decided to head to the Kultur Park to see if I could place a tent for the night. I arrived, found the security box, and approached to ask if I could camp. I already knew the answer as I had asked previously. They tried to call their supervisor, but there was no answer. 'Behind the tower', they told me.

It was good enough for me. I headed around behind the large structure to find a secluded area. When I say 'secluded', it was fairly open but there were trees scattered throughout to provide some form of protection.

A short period passed. Actually, as I had placed my bicycle on the ground and took off the backpack from my shoulders, another security guard on an electric scooter drove past, stopped, stared at me, and drove in to have a word. They spoke very broken english; I spoke no Turkish. The answer was no, I could not camp there. They then showed me and told me that when I travelled, I should always be careful with items of value. They then pulled out a switchblade to show me how they would protect themselves.

I laughed.

I was still unsure whether I could place my tent for the night. About ten minutes had passed, and they were on their second lap of the park. I was still unsure. They were a strange character. They even got out a translator, but that was just awkward. Some Turkish people were too friendly. Don't know if that is the correct word to describe them. Maybe *open* is a better word. The security guard left me to it.

I noticed another guard on patrol and decided to ask them whether I can camp. This person could speak english quite well. Again, I knew what the answer was, but I continued to ask. Their manager happened to be on a scooter driving past. The guard stopped them and chatted to them in Turkish. Success, I could camp for the night. The area was right at the front of the park with the Atatürk Monument in full view.

I felt like a VIP, being given one of the nicest spots to camp in the whole park—a view of the hills with a large Turkish flag and lights from the houses flickering against the flag, with the wind creating an ambient effect. Also, a restaurant was playing fifties music, and I enjoyed every track; it was rather soothing to listen to before going to bed.

Earlier on that night, I befriended a little kitten. I gave it some meat I had, but that wasn't enough for the puss. I offered it bread, and it thought I had more meat; therefore, it did not eat. It continued to be very friendly and was purring, which was nice to hear. I gave the kitten the attention it deserved. I put my hand into my backpack and poked about for more food. I found a Turkish Laughing Cow triangle. I opened it and tasted a piece, no good for me alone. If only I had more bread and meat to put it in a sandwich. I placed the triangle on the ground, and the kitten began to chow down, purring more heavily.

Another cat came over, scoping out the tent and the kitten. I continued to stroke the kitten. The cat began to play the cute card and started rolling about the grass, looking for attention. This is how they lure people in with food and affection, I reckon. It was funny to watch as I had no more food to give that night. Another cat walking past made a swipe at the cat, I assumed out of jealousy. I hissed in their direction, and the cat made tracks across the park.

Time to get ready for bed. I placed my secondary bag out for the kitten as it may have wanted to sleep in the tent. I left the tent open slightly, in case the kitten decided to come in. I thought about mosquitos entering the tent, but then if the kitten was there, it would be rewarded with a small protein snack. The kitten entered, checking out the perimeter before lying down on the bag.

Before bed, I drank two flasks of water. The classical music put me to sleep, and I had a great sleep until the sun rose in the morning, and I was awakened. Time to get up. I packed up my belongings and was off to the masjid to clean for the day.

That morning, I was supposed to head to the retail store at nine thirty for commission work, I do believe. I thought I may have had too much water last night and overslept, though I hadn't taken the work seriously. When I went into the masjid, I was ushered out by the cleaner. I decided to leave my backpack there as it was a place of worship, and I doubted anyone would steal from there; plus, it'd be there when I returned, and I had all my valuables.

Off to the centre I went. I decided to stop at a McDonald's for a cone and then another before heading off towards the bazaar as I was in no hurry. Before I entered the bazaar, I locked up my bicycle on the high street as this was not a social visit. Every other time, I had arrived with my bicycle and backpack, not today. I was there to collect money which I had lent to someone when we went out on Saturday night.

Luckily, they were there this time, and I was adamant that I would be getting my money that day as I wanted to leave this place. They were speaking with someone. I gave them the time before we talked. I was asked into a separate shop and offered tea while they talked business. I was there to collect money out of principle. I did not like being sent home the previous day as they were not there because of a toothache. I should have been out of İzmir several days previously. I left the bazaar thanking all those who I spoke to and offered me jars of water. I felt good.

It was midday by this stage; there was a slim chance I would be leaving now. I found a restaurant to refuel and planned a way out of İzmir. Afterwards, I headed to the masjid to digest, reflect, meditate, and sleep. When

I first arrived, I noticed that my backpack was no longer there. I didn't panic. I would have been happy to lose my backpack, although there would be several items there which would have been hard to replace, but where would I sleep while I travelled without the tent? At the same time, I knew I left my backpack in a safe place and that it would not be far. I decided to have a look, but all the rooms within the enclosure were locked.

The only reason I came across the masjid was that I needed the toilet, and a sign pointed me there. When I arrived, I noticed a nice varnished wooden door with shoes outside. I opened the door to see what was inside—carpeted room, plenty of space, religious symbols, books on Islam, and a varnished staircase/podium. This would be a space where I could come to sit and relax away from the city; the main attraction was the carpet. Eventually, the cleaner came along and showed me to my backpack, and away I went in search of the next place that I was to be going. I even stopped into a bicycle shop to get air in the tyres as I like my tyres solid for riding. That evening, I could honestly say that I had no intention of cycling. I had stayed longer than I had imagined. I had never planned to stay there as long as I had. To me, it was just another city on the map, another city by the sea, nothing special. But I was not sure if everything was fully authentic in Turkey. You could buy a branded T-shirt for twenty Turkish lira, about six pound sterling. Back home, you would pay nearly forty pound sterling for the same T-shirt, though when you looked at the label, it said 'Made in Turkey'. I was unsure how it all worked and whether it was counterfeit. How could that be possible? Turkey must have some relaxed laws regarding this.

Anyway, I had no intention of cycling yet. I felt that İzmir had drained much of the energy out of this soul. I had planned on finding a truck that would take me to either Istanbul or Ankara as I needed to find an embassy to speak to them about the next country I hoped to visit.

A few nights previous, when trying to find the stadium from a different direction, I came across a truck stop which I used as a starting point for trying to secure a lift. I called into the truck stop. I approached several people sitting at a table, drinking tea, and chatting. They pointed me to a seat, and I sat down. I explained where I wanted to go. They didn't really understand, and I was offered a cup of tea. The people began to understand after I showed them my signs. They grabbed a flashlight and began asking several drivers if they were going my direction but no such luck.

The main person asked if I was hungry. I should have said no but said yes. They were of Syrian origin and had been in Turkey the last year or so. I didn't ask many more questions as there was a reason they had left, and well, I didn't need to know that. They went into the office, grabbed a long cushion from their sofa, and gave it to me to lie on for the night. They pointed to a trailer. 'You sleep there,' they said. They then set up an area where I could sleep.

I set up my tent. I put it on the trailer, and away to sleep I went. I had a great sleep.

That morning, I was awakened at twenty past five. I thought it was time to go and there was a truck waiting.

No, I was being asked to leave, not quite sure why, but I was ready. The first place I would look would be the first truck stop when I entered.

I followed the road into İzmir; from there, I had no such luck. I found another truck stop, and I asked—no luck. One of the workers there redirected me towards Port D, which was a place to look. I headed over and had looked about the large shipping port. I showed my signs with no luck. A few nearly stopped, but most were having none of it. I decided to call it a day and headed to the bus station to check the times and price of a bus to Ankara. If reasonable, I would pay.

Five kilometres later, I arrived. It was a busy place, mostly with salespeople though. I asked. I was not quite sure what I heard, but I handed over fifteen Turkish lira and thought it was a bargain. 'No, fifty lira', said the attendant. I had a quick think and did my calculation, about fifteen pound sterling for six hundred kilometres. I pondered— only fifteen pound sterling. I did want out of İzmir.

'Bus in ten minutes!' someone yelled.

'Thank you, sir,' I said, and to the bus I went.

I boarded the bus, and before I knew it, the bus journey was over. My time on the bus was a mixture of sleep and contemplation. Should I try to get a lift on the same bus back to İzmir and begin from there? It would count against using no public transport on my travels, though that was not too important to me. At least in Ankara, I can apply for visas. I pondered, and then I slept. I did hope I could return to Izmir.

Why did I get the bus in the first place? Mainly because there was one in ten minutes, and that would help me progress and get back on the road. I felt like I had cheated. I did not think I was ready to leave the comfort of the city so abruptly. Had I cheated? Not really. This was not a test, though public transport was never on my agenda. Once, I took public transport, six hundred kilometres for fifteen pound sterling, and I am okay with that. Turkey has been a challenge.

Why did I ever go to İzmir in the first place? Simply because I changed my plan from heading through Istanbul at a very short notice; I never planned it, though I decided to head there and see what it was about. It definitely had an appeal to a younger audience; therefore, the lift from roughly the Turkish border was perfect. When entering Turkey, there was a crossroads. Straight on led you to Istanbul. Right led you to İzmir. Left led you to İpsala.

Things from here on in were going to be tough. And well, they were not. That night, I found a grassy area next to the bus terminal. When I said 'found', it was not hard to see. I headed over to the terminal where the buses entered and exited. I approached the security box which was manned by several people. I asked a person if I could place a tent in the area, signalling using my hands as usual. They did not understand my clever hand signals.

One of them pulled out a phone and signalled to wait a few seconds, I assumed to get out Google Translate. I was right. I typed, 'Sir, is it okay if I place my tent on the grassy area until morning out of view from passing automobiles?' They signalled for me to wait, called a colleague, and handed me the phone.

'Hello?' I heard from an Asian voice.

A few buses passed, and I found it very hard to hear the person. Several minutes passed, and I could not comprehend or understand what had been said. Basically, I could not camp there, and the security guards did not have the authority to let me. I then drew a picture of a tent in a field. They confirmed the information with one another, and one took the drawing pad and wrote '100m'.

I followed the instructions, and I came to the end of the road and found an embankment beside a university. I set up camp and did the usual pre-bed activities, and off to bed I went. That night, I had a great undisturbed sleep; about thirteen hours was had, though I did not feel fresh waking up in the capital. I packed up camp and headed towards the terminal.

The place was massive, three stories high, with over sixty terminals and sixty bus companies all wanting your money. It was busy; it felt like a market. I walked around the building and found nothing of interest; you had to pay for everything, from the Internet to the toilet. People made their small money from the visiting people, though it would all add up. The people who worked at the bathrooms probably received buttons for their noble work while the owners reaped all the benefits of such a basic necessity. I was only there to wash myself and brush my teeth, although the toilet attendant noticed me leaving, and I tried to explain. They were not very old, probably a teenager. They hadn't demanded; they asked. I said I had no Turkish lira, which was true. I had just arrived, and I said I would be back later.

After this, I headed outside with a map that I had received from a tourist information office as well as the location of the Iranian Embassy. I asked for directions as I literally had no idea where I was or what main road was in front of me. I set off down the road in search of the embassy. I was on the right road, a quick turn down a set of steps to change onto another highway. Several exits later, I asked for help. 'Where am I exactly?' I was at the right place. I just had to head up the road about a hundred metres.

I arrived outside the embassy. I quickly changed my T-shirt, lengthened my shorts, and headed in after I pressed the buzzer of course. I waited until the people in front were finished with the receptionist, and I thought about my chosen attire and hoped that it was not disrespectful or offensive as my calves were out. Time for me to check in. I handed over my passport, and I was asked to take a ticket. I headed into a crowded room of people, who were waiting on their applications, most smartly dressed. I probably looked out of place as usual, but what did that matter? I may never see these people again.

In a matter of time, I was called forwards, and I handed over my passport. 'Do you have a reference number?' said the attendant.

'What reference number?' I said, puzzled.

'The one when you apply for a visa', they said.

'First I have heard of this, first-time applicant', I responded.

The clerk advised that I go to a travel agent and apply through them. That was us finished; out the door I went. When inside, I asked the receptionist where to find a travel agent; they handed me a piece of paper of one not far away, just down Atatürk Boulevard where the embassy was located at the time.

I reached the block of offices, about six stories high. I got strange looks from the attendant. 'Iran visa?' they said knowingly. They signalled upstairs and around. I knew what they meant, but I wasn't quite sure where exactly. It'd be best to investigate.

I saw the office but continued on up to see what else was there and to confirm it was said office. I headed in. 'Apply for a visa for Iran?' I said to the attendant.

I filled out a form. What would I put as my occupation? Designer or traveller? I would have happily put traveller, but I wondered what the foreign minister would think if they saw there was a traveller from Ireland applying for a visa to Iran. I scribbled that out and stuck with designer, an occupation all the same, unlike traveller, although that was my occupation at the time.

The clerk was doing the paperwork. I asked to use the Wi-Fi, and I was connected to high-speed wireless for the next twenty minutes. I went onto Ireland's Department of Foreign Affairs website to let them know there was an Irish citizen heading to Iran, just to let them know. Even on their website, they expected people to inform them. Then there was the payment of fifty US dollars. All I had was fifty Turkish lira. I tried to use my debit card with no luck. They got another money machine from downstairs from another vendor, which was a success.

Now all I had to do was wait ten working days to get a reference number—a scam if you asked me. Now I was one step closer to getting towards my next country.

Previously, when I had left the embassy and was unlocking the bicycle, a wasp came over ever so ferociously and stung out of nowhere. It must have been the foreign skin that they were attracted to or that I was unlucky. Luckily, it was only one and not the whole swarm that were hovering behind the wall. I hadn't been stung since I was fourteen, right on the back of the head that time, and the countless times before that. I hate wasps when they sting—grimness.

And then the weather started to change, though it was terrible outside on the bus towards Ankara with the thunder and lightning. Again, I began to think that I was not supposed to be here this quickly, same with Kavala— too much travel, not enough cycle.

I found a cafe, had a jug of water, and pondered. Next thing I knew, I was on the bicycle and heading back to the bus station—for good reasons as well. I had decided to head back to İzmir to begin cycling as I did not give it a real start. Ticket was arranged when I reached the terminal. I went back to the kiosk to change the ticket to early morning. Then it came to me. Why was I heading back to İzmir? I had fast-tracked to there. I had made the decision to change the ticket once again back to İpsala near the border where I could begin cycling once again, taking my time, not pushing myself too much. The farthest I could get with the money I had was Tekirdağ, about one hundred kilometres from İpsala.

I waited several hours before the bus departed. I said 'waited'. I enjoyed my time there speaking to random people, and I enjoyed the indoors. I even spoke with someone from Iraq who showed me a video of themselves firing a gun in their apartment building. I came across a book kiosk, and I saw a sudoku book for two Turkish lira; unfortunately, I only had one. The person would not accept. I saw several defaced books and made the purchase.

Handy, now I can exercise my brain as I travel. Before that, the same teenager from the morning escapades at the toilet was walking past, and I offered them the money for the facility, but they did not want it anymore—good person. That was how I was able to purchase the sudoku.

It was time to board the bus. I sat down the back, and the driver came down to check everyone's ticket. I was moved a few seats forwards beside a flamboyant Turkish person. They were unsteady the whole journey and even invited me to listen to music with them. No thanks. I would prefer to sit in silence than listen to Aqua. Time passed, and they got off the bus into the pouring rain, leaving the double seater to myself—feet up and sleep time. Eventually, the bus arrived at Tekirdağ.

The bus station was a ghost station at this time, not a person in sight. I headed across the road to place the tent for the night. A taxi driver asked if I wanted to stay in the depot—friendliness of the Turkish. I set up my tent in no time and slept the night away until being awoken by another Turkish person telling me it was time to get up—again, another friendly person. They even showed me where I could wash. Then I disassembled my tent, and off I went to the bus station to find a bus to İpsala.

The bus was sorted, though not easily as I had no money, and the closest cash machine was several kilometres away. When I made the purchase, I was unsure if the ticket was real, or maybe it was just the language barrier. I waited until being directed towards a bus for İpsala. There were no seat numbers; therefore, I could lie in peace and complete a puzzle, though there were two biddies in front slightly distracting me from the puzzle, but I completed it, and the energy was drained from my body. I had to train more.

It was a usual bus journey, nothing to complain about. I arrived in İpsala, a place I was thirteen days ago. It was an odd number, unlucky for some; luckily, I don't believe in that superstition. If it was meant to be, it was meant to be.

Off the bus I went. Bicycle out, and it was time to find water after that journey. No joy. I looked at the back tyre, and it was almost flat. It'd be best to pump it up slightly before I headed down the road.

Ready to roll to the next stopping station, I passed a park; this was where I would have lunch and fix my tyre. Down the road, I came across a Kipa Extra. I had no idea. In I went and picked up supplies, and I was back to the bicycle. Flat tyre? No bother. It had been needing repaired the last number days, same with the front. To the park I went.

I found a picnic table in the shade, prepared food, and then emptied the contents of my backpack as I knew I was going to have to begin cycling again after the midday sun died down. I looked at everything that I had, the largest items being the tent, sleeping bag, mat, and pillow. Two I acquired along the way, two conveniences. I didn't know how long I would keep them. And the rest was made up of clothing, cycling-related matter, toiletries, and fire charger. All these would need to be replaced eventually if I decided to chuck.

There was a passer-by. I asked them if they knew where to find a flask of water in İpsala. They were unable to help me in my quest. Back to my table I went. Time to fix my tyre. This time like no other, I removed the valve first and then remembered where the thorn was; therefore, I did not need water to fix the puncture.

I left that to dry.

I noticed two people setting up a picnic, and then another person and several other people arrived on a Friday afternoon. They must be retired or were pulling a sickie at work. I didn't understand how they can enjoy their Friday like this, although they were two and a half times older than myself. Fair play to them.

After a final check on my tyre, we were golden. My backpack was prepared. *Am I ready? I suppose, I would have to be!*

TURKEY PART TWO

On the bicycle I went, taking it easy, one kilometre at a time—piece of cake. I was up the first hill and down the same. This was the pattern throughout the cycling I had done in Turkey, similar to Albania, but that was much tougher.

I was speeding down a hill, and I noticed people sitting outside a teahouse. I threw my hand up to signal I was having a great time. A few of them waved. I heard one shout something. I stopped the bicycle, turned around, and approached the table.

One of them responded and pointed to a seat.

I described my story using hand signals. After a short period, I was left at the table, and tea arrived. It was not my fault that I don't speak Turkish.

Previously just as I was starting on the road, several military vehicles passed with two shiny double-barrelled-mortar-looking weapons, and I didn't think they were for scaring away birds. They could do damage. I wondered what they were preparing for. It was none of my business.

I set off on the bicycle, waving to those around— you know, like a friendly chap or an arrogant, dare I say it, tourist. These roads were tough. I cycled sixty-five kilometres before calling it a night. Nothing eventful happened that Friday night. The highlight was watching a person feed a herd of sheep and being barked at by the same person's dog.

It was funny; many dogs had chased me on the bicycle. They ran side by side, barking but never biting— yet. They had the chance to bite, but they never take that chance.

That night, I had a decent sleep, though it was cold, a foetal position was posed throughout the night to keep warm. I woke up to the tent being drenched in dew. The sun quickly dried that out. I set off up the road, not sure why I didn't camp at the top of the hill apart from the fact I was wrecked, and it was getting late. I still had thirty-five kilometres to Tekirdağ, which meant I definitely cycled sixty-five kilometres yesterday after I returned to near the border of Turkey.

I continued to cycle, finally reaching the small municipality. I went in search of a market. I saw a sign on the other side of a road for one. I crossed the road, only to find an empty shop. Towards the centre I went. I saw a mosque and decided to hide out there for a period. I was able to give my feet a good scrub using the water provided from the taps out the front. I entered the sanctuary. There was a person hoovering. When they finished, the person said, 'Are you a tourist?'

'No', I replied.

'Are you a Muslim?' said the person.

'No', I replied.

They then invited me into their office with a co-worker. We chatted, and it felt like a recruitment meeting. I was wearing shorts and T-shirt. They asked me to come back in twenty minutes for a jug of water. They must be changing tactics. I complied. I heard my name being called. I headed towards the office, and I had a nice jug of water and several different types of biscuits before the people headed home.

At this time, I was still evading the midday sun. I headed into the comfortable zone to meditate and lie down, eventually leaving as people entered to pray. I put on my sandals, and on the bicycle I went towards Istanbul. One of the good things about cycling the national roads was there was usually an indication of how far it was to the next destination—handy. But the speedometer worked perfectly as well in gauging kilometres cycled as not all roads had the distance.

I cycled about eighty kilometres before braking for proper food at a beach resort. I noticed sunbeds, and experience taught me you usually have to pay to sit. I asked. 'Go on ahead,' said the attendant.

I ate my food and was ready to leave, but I needed water. I asked the same person for water. We began to chat. They were from Syria and had been here one month. Good for them. They offered me a tea. I accepted. A customer came over to use the shower. They asked me if I needed a shower. I didn't hesitate, and a shower was had.

Off down the road I went. I cycled another twenty kilometres before seeing a cliff where I wanted to place the tent for the evening. Definitely the best view I have had on my travels thus far. Pity there were boats, but surely, it was only natural in this day and age.

I found a person. 'Can I camp here?' I asked. They didn't speak a word of english but could growl. I checked the area, and I saw no one in the house behind me—campsite found. I tried to ask to see if I could camp with no luck of an answer. I set up camp, and I prepared food and wrote.

Previously, someone was waiting for a lift. I put out my fist, and there was a connection. A great feeling of power was transferred between the two fists.

That morning, I awakened after having a great sleep. I was fresh but not ready to leave; this had been the nicest spot I had camped in throughout my travels. I was in no real hurry to leave, and I may stay here another night. If only there was more water. I survived. I was content with what I had, and I would find more in the morning. *Cycling can wait until then*, I thought, though I was not completely certain.

Today was a day of rest, and I took that literally. I would always try to keep my day of rest free from cycling and find a nice place to camp and, well, recuperate. I would hopefully be on the road from six o'clock in the morning to eight o'clock at night with enough rest in between, though I had no alarm—fingers crossed—not that it mattered. I would awaken when I had had adequate rest. I awakened at seven o'clock and set off on the bicycle towards Istanbul.

I was not sure of the exact places in between; I was just following the highway. That night, I reached another area by the beach, hopped over a fence into a new building, and placed my tent inside on the second floor. I awakened from the beach-view house I had acquired the previous night and had a big yawn while looking out into the ocean and was back on the road to Istanbul, only another forty kilometres to go.

The kilometres were dropping, and I saw the Istanbul skyline changing in the distance as well as the large road ahead of me which I had to climb. It was best to drop it down a number of gears. I thought that this hill was the most intense, most power driven hill that I had encountered. There was not a single cyclist in sight at the time.

I was on the main road which had changed into a four-lane highway all of a sudden. I continued to the top and thought that I was in the centre. I hopped off the bicycle and used a bridge to cross to the other side of the road to use the facilities at the shopping mall and get the bearings right. I came across another masjid. Great, time for sleep and clearing of the mind, not that one needed to; but then while cycling into the unknown, you needed to prepare mentally, a little bit, sort of, not really. I was determined—determined to see how far I can cycle and travel in one year. July to July would be ideal. I would have already been seven days past Istanbul if it wasn't for İzmir. Bad decision all in all. Winter was coming. I needed to find myself in a warmer climate, though that was later on down the line.

I was trying to navigate myself out of Istanbul. It felt like I had been cycling for days when I had not. These hills/inclines and highways take it out of you. Earlier on that day when at the top of the hill, I noticed a Turkish person under a tree mixing drinks. I hopped over the fence and approached as I needed to lighten the load on my shoulders. I emptied the contents of my backpack to see what I could give the person. The person didn't speak english, but my meaning was understood. Anyway, I was lightening the load and gave them a decent green cotton T-shirt that was useless to me as, when washing it, the water would soak the T-shirt and would take too long to dry. It was in great condition. They were happy for it.

Then I pulled out my Philips electric razor. I thought about this for a while only because I had it the past five years and was still getting use of it; it had served me well. I pondered and then eventually gave the person the razor as I needed to prepare for the next country. A baby face may not be as acceptable as a half-grown beard in the Islamic Republic. Next were a pair of black shoes, which I was very reluctant to give; by the time I had made a decision, they were gone. The person gave me a load of grapes, a few bottles of water, and a bottle of fizzy juice.

I sat there and thought how I could make this a purer travel session. Today out of choice, I had stuck to a diet of mostly bread and wholemeal biscuits as well as water. All the meat I had been consuming I didn't believe to be healthy. At one stage, I had a cooking tray; replacing it would cost me money. And when I thought about it, it wasn't taking up that much room or weight, but it was hard to clean when you don't have a reasonable supply of water as water was utilised for more important processes.

While at the roadside spot, there was a wild kitten roaming; the person disliked the creature, the kitten. Yes, I did try to catnap. This cat was wild, playful. It did not want to enter my backpack—well, it did, but it did not want to stay there. I tried twice; the third time, the cat ran away. There goes another broken heart.

Off down the road I went, catless but a little lighter. Eventually, I came off the road because of my energy levels. I stopped at the side of the road for a quick snack. On the road I continued. It was starting to get dark, and there was a stream of traffic which stretched for many kilometres; it was bumper to bumper. I set off luckily at the top of the hill, a rolling start, the way I liked it.

Eventually, I came to the area where it was most crammed. There were Turkish people on the highway selling various goods. There was no fresh water, only bottled. I ended up buying a bottle from one of the people in the street as I had left my water bottle at the kitten spot. I was slightly annoyed when I realised it, but there was no chance I was going back for it. 'No going back' was a motto I was trying to live by as I travelled. Only recently had it come into play, although if it was of great importance such as a passport, then I returned to the scene.

I passed more sellers, many of them. I began to make noise as I cycled past; they all loved it and began yelling and shouting in the street, and then I was gone. I came towards a road which was jammed. I could see the Bosporus Bridge in the distance.

Before I headed, I did notice a sign, one with a car on a green background, similar to the one that I saw outside Karlovy Vary in the Czech Republic. It would be best to ignore that sign and keep on going. I continued, but I was stopped by the traffic police. 'You cannot cycle here,' they said.

'Okay', I responded.

They cleared off to deal with another matter. They spotted me again and flagged me over. 'Sir, you cannot go here,' they told me.

I waited, and then all of a sudden, the bus in front opened the doors, and all the passengers got out. *Strange*, I thought. Another bus pulled up which was empty. I hopped on that bus, continued over the bridge, and got off a few stops after. I was very lucky. But I didn't know where I was. I had a rough idea, but I needed Internet to tell me exactly where I was.

I headed off down the road, and I saw a cafe. I asked to use their Wi-Fi, but there was none. They found a person who could speak english instead. They called a friend on the telephone. I spoke to them and handed the phone back. 'You want Turkish tea?' said the attendant.

By this stage, a small crowd gathered as I asked how to get back to the national road that would take me through the country. Google Translate was opened. Then an english-speaking Turkish person arrived who was able to direct me onto the national road as well as plan a route out for me. It wasn't too hard to plan a route using the map of Turkey that I had. I was to follow the road one thousand, two hundred kilometres to Erzurum. 'Follow blue signs, not green,' one person told me.

'I understand,' I replied.

'Green equals motorway,' they told me.

I cycled towards the old national road. I cycled onto it, and it still felt like a motorway. I continued, but it was getting late. I headed off the road and cycled around two hundred metres, and noticed a grassy plain that would be perfect to camp. I turned back and decided to ask two Turkish people sitting outside a cabin if it would be okay to place a tent there, even though it was not their land. They didn't really understand. I continued on anyway, jumping over two fences and began to place my tent. One got a flashlight and pointed it in my direction. 'No, no!' they shouted over. Luckily, I followed as there were a few Alsatians in the compound. Now I understood why I could not camp there. I wasn't sure if they were wild dogs or guard dogs. It'd be best to leave the site.

The person spoke to another at the main road who pointed to the pavement. I could sleep on the pavement apparently. I thanked the people for their time and headed off. I cycled half a kilometre before I found an abandoned house. I checked it out, but it reeked of waste. I headed around the back to an abandoned area with several trees. This would do rightly, and off to sleep I went.

That morning, I awakened to the sound of thunder and lightning. I stayed put in the tent; the water was dripping in through the single layer. I had found in these sorts of bad weather conditions that it was best to curl up in a ball and wait for it to pass. And it passed. I even got a few extra hours of sleep—bonus. By the time I was up, the sun was well and truly high in the sky; it was about eleven o'clock in the morning. I had time to sketch and pack up my belongings.

Today I had my first bicycle crash, about two thousand kilometres later on the hard shoulder. I mustn't have been paying attention to how close I was to the side of the road where there were signs. Then all of a sudden, I found myself on the road, sprawled out like a starfish. I had a look and noticed there was a sign sticking out. It must have hit the bicycle on the right-hand side handlebar. I peeled myself up off the ground. It was nothing serious. There were a few grazes on the bicycle. I was also grazed but was grand. I headed off the road to inspect the bicycle, and everything was in order. I felt slightly dizzy. I saw a food stand and fruit stand behind me and had food to correct the dizziness. I ate two portions of egg fried rice and purchased oranges for the day. I needed water.

I headed on the national road towards Ankara. I still felt slightly offbeat. After sixteen kilometres, I stopped at a shopping outlet mainly to get water. I walked in; like all malls I had been in, less than a handful, they had security guards at the entrance, metal detectors, and an X-ray machine. It was a bit extreme for a mall, but surely, they can do what they want. Who knew what maniacs were at these days? I headed through with my backpack, took it off, and it was X-rayed. 'Can I leave the backpack here?' I said. I got the usual head tilt and 'tut' and away I went.

There was nothing really in here for me. I headed around and looked for water. I came across a Kipa and walked around, browsing the store, looking for water and a baking tray half the size for cooking over a fire. I headed to the counter to pay for my water, but the PIN was declined. What a pity. And I was taking a break from the Internet for a while; therefore, I wouldn't be able to look at the current state of my student account. It was probably all these charges I had been receiving abroad!

I headed past a window and could see that it was lashing from the heavens. Not time to leave yet. I headed outside where there was shelter. I started speaking to a tall person, and we chatted. They were an ex-boxer-politician-bodyguard apparently. They let me punch them, they were solid. I got bored of standing around and decided to head to the bathroom to put on my wetsuit, which consisted of an anorak and 'Mac in a Sac' trousers—great choice for the wild weather that was happening outside. Hands were shook, and away I went.

I returned to the bicycle. It had changed position, and some pest had turned on the lights—well, at least they didn't steal them. A security guard came over and told me I cannot park here. 'Yes, I am on my bicycle though. Goodbye,' I said from the saddle as I glided away into the mist.

The rain had died down, though still there. I progressed onwards. I felt I had reached closer to the mainland. I passed several shipping yards and freight container warehouses.

The rain was getting heavier. I felt alive. Bombing down a steep incline at fifty kilometres per hour, it was time to put on the brakes. This could get dangerous very quickly. My bicycle and I sped through. It was the only bicycle on the road. The rain really gave me the necessary energy that was needed for the day.

Along the road, I stopped at a hotel for water. 'Large or small?' said the attendant.

'Just a bottle, please', I said.

The person returned with a bottle, and away I went. 'Thank you, kind person,' I said from the saddle.

I continued along the road, and the rain was still there with no sign of shifting. In the distance, I could see an opening in the sky. It'd best to head there. The energy I had got me singing, 'Singing a song on the national road, riding along the national road, the national road, cycling along, grooming my beard, on the national road.' I had many others lyrics that fanatically got me through the afternoon. This was a great cycle.

Then I stopped at a petrol station, and I asked a person if they would have a glass of water. They handed me a pack, and I only took one as that was all I needed. How very thoughtful though. Then I headed around the front of the garage. I noticed hot water, and I asked if it was free. 'You want tea or coffee?' they asked. 'Coffee', I replied. Nothing like a hot coffee in the rain. That warmed me up and ready for round two.

While there, people came over asking for a video supporting their local team. I accepted and rambled off what they said to me for a bit of craic. They were happy about it.

On the way to İzmit I went. There was nothing to see there. I continued onwards towards Sakarya. I saw a sign and decided to take a break as I needed water. As I sat on a chain outside a market, I could feel splatters of rain. I finished up, and into the storm I went. It got late; the shower was on for hours to come.

I passed several abandoned buildings where I could place the tent for the night. I stopped at one where I would place the tent under shelter. I checked the door of the building, but it was locked. I headed around the back, and there was shelter provided by a small roof—success. I began to assemble the tent. I heard a car stop out the front. I noticed flashlights, and I heard talking. It'd be best to head around and see what the commotion was. Lights were pointed on me. It'd be best to raise my hands as my intentions were simple. Guns were pointed at me, I am near sure. The person pulled out a badge. It was the police. This could be bad, trespassing or worse. These two officers were looking for trouble. I, being a noble person, completely complied with them and more.

'You missed three pockets,' I said after they had searched me.

They headed around the back, and they saw my backpack, emptied it completely, and found nothing. They saw my tent and laughed. 'Tourist', they said. And away they went. It was the second sighting of the police on my travels. Not since the Czech Republic had I had run-ins with the law. I hoped this was not a sign of things to come.

I finished off the assembly of the tent. I left the waterproofs outside to dry, and into the tent I went for sleep. That morning, I awakened at eleven o'clock. This would be one of my latest starts; some would say I was off to a bad start. I would have cycled about two kilometres, and I heard a 'click-clack' from the gearing system. I looked down, and the chain had snapped. Now instead of stopping where I had heard the noise, I continued and then backtracked, looking for the parts of the chain—no luck finding all the pieces. Only the split link was found, not all the corresponding parts. Up and down I walked along the national road. I found two washers that sat in between two adjacent chain pieces. I continued on looking, but they were not in sight.

I walked to Sakarya. I entered the city with a population of half a million. There were two small villages of mechanic shops on either side of the road, about one hundred of them. Finding a bicycle shop was tough enough, especially while wearing a Croatian jersey. Eventually, I was told to go across the road; this was the third person who gave me directions, and I believed them. Across the road I went. I asked a mechanic, and they asked a person to show me where to go. I thanked them, but the place was closed.

I saw a person on a bicycle carrying about twenty bottles of water and a container filled with a white product, possibly yoghurt or milk. Anyway, the person brought me towards the bicycle shop, which was full of old bicycles needing repairs. They got a tin, poured it out onto a newspaper, and found the parts that were needed for the repair. They fixed the chain within two minutes. I was amazed. That process I could not have completed as I did not have the necessary tools; next time, I may be more prepared. I learnt something that day. The person didn't charge me for the repair, a kind Turkish person.

I headed off into the city centre to find a bank to change my euro to Turkish lira as it would be necessary as I travelled through the country. And when was I going to need euro? I planned to leave Europe as soon as I can—well, as long as it would take, possibly another thousand kilometres or around six hundred miles.

Now I had Turkish lira again. I have always had money, though at some stage the money would run out. I try to extend the life, but I always—well, not always, but I don't choose the wisest of foods or activities. I hoped to change this pattern. Earlier, I found one Turkish lira in my tent, the same lira I had planned on using to buy water the previous day at the shopping mall, the same lira I had went to bed with; but I was not going to pull out my tent and search for it in the supermarket. Water can always be found. I stopped off at a market, purchased two eggs, took a cup and a fork, and mixed, and then I added water and drank—a healthy option. Now that I had Turkish lira, I found a bread stand, and five loaves were purchased. I ate one and headed towards the entrance of the town.

I walked past a cooking store denominated by the cooking gear that was on show. I called in, looking for a metal plate to cook my eggs and various meats on. I had a look about the shop, but everything was too expensive. I approached the kiosk, and a person shook my hand, a pleasant gesture. I explained and drew a picture of what I was looking for. They understood and showed me to the metal plates—success. I can now cook my own food with the help of my friend, fire. I found a supermarket to purchase meat and other necessities for the day as I planned to have a feast that night.

With the shopping done, it was time to find a park for lunch. I found one. Well, I passed what looked like a park on the way in. I did a quick lap, and there was no sign of anywhere to sit for lunch. A security guard signalled over as I was passing. 'You want tea?' they asked.

'Okay', I replied. Nothing like a free cup of tea.

I locked up my bicycle and made a sandwich. They came back, and we headed towards the cafe. Tea was had, and I was given another, and then the same waiter offered me a jug of water. Great. I was not sure how long I spent there; football was on, and it would be rude to head after my drinks. My belongings were in a safe place in the security office. Eventually, I asked to get my backpack. Hands were shook, and away I went in search of Düzce.

Now I would have been there already if it wasn't for my chain, which set me up for a bad day. I was happy to take my time and was rewarded with tea. I set off, maintaining a speed of twenty-five kilometres per hour; after that hour, I was burnt out, from twenty-five to sixteen kilometres per hour. I stopped to eat to return the energy levels transferred into the machine that was the bicycle, and then I was on the road for another ten kilometres before making camp at the top of a mount far away from passing vehicles. I had no fire tonight, though, maybe in the morning.

No fire was had, and everything around the camp was soaking with dew that had accumulated from the previous night. It was a cold night, but I slept well.

Off I walked down the hill with the bicycle in hand to prevent a puncture. I climbed hills and went down hills all the way to Düzce. Off the main road I went to pick up supplies for the day. I had my usual protein shake consisting of eggs and water, which would do me for a period. I kept an egg as I planned to cook that night using the hot plate. Off I went towards Bolu, only thirty kilometres. It shouldn't take me too long. In the distance, I could see massive hills. It'd be best to stop for proper food before I ascended.

I ascended on the mountain, which had about a ten percent incline, for about thirty kilometres. Why do they do this? Well, it was a mountain. Off I went into a cafe for water. On the bicycle again, I climbed several kilometres before asking a parked driver for a lift. I took my lift, and I sat back and enjoyed the view; it was an intensive week of cycling. I passed Bolu and saw signs for my next vantage point, Gerende.

I stopped off at a shop for supplies; upon entry, I saw watermelons that looked battered. I saw a sign saying '1 TL'—excellent, a melon for that price. I picked up a melon and headed to the counter to pay as well as picking up other supplies such as bread. When I went to pay, it turned out it was one Turkish lira per kilogram. I even had to pull out a pen and paper to show the calculations of the groceries.

Problem resolved, I left with bread and several nectarines. If the price for the melon was as noted, I would have eaten it out the front of the store as my backpack was uncomfortably heavy already.

Off I went on my bicycle towards my next destination. I climbed, eventually coming to a very sweet spot to camp for the night. I found wood, dug a hole, and added wood. I had two matches left—match one, fail; match two, fail. I went to my backpack to get a lighter which had no flint. I had a third match which had the smallest amount of powder; I used this to try to ignite the lighter. No flame, no fire. I forgot about the fire and headed for sleep. This had been the second best place I had camped. It was up high, with the mountains in sight; pity about the fire. It was definitely windier on higher levels.

In the morning, I awakened of my own accord, without a farmer telling me to get off their property or anything, pure powerful. The sun was beaming through, though not as rampant as throughout my travels; it was heating me up slightly. Time to arise, do my morning business, and be back on the road. Off down the hill I went onto the national road.

In a matter of time, I arrived in Gerende. I headed into the *şehir merkezi* to find a shop to purchase supplies for the day, and I was back on the road. I stopped at the side of the road on a grassy plain surrounded by a stone wall. I sat down and prepared my breakfast and lunch. I looked at the map to see where my next destination would be as I was not going back to the capital. There was nothing there for me, just an embassy. I continued to head east. Winter was coming. I needed to be somewhere south but first east to take me through to warmer climates. Turkey was getting cold at night; it reminded me of Ireland in winter.

I was heading for the place of Çerkeş. The road was starting with an incline of about three percent, not too bad. I continued on the road, which was fierce, like most of the roads in Turkey that I had cycled on. I eventually made a stop and spoke with two people working at the side of the road. One of them spoke a reasonable level of english. They were picking mushrooms up the mountain for their family tea.

I left the people to it as they were off to a local mosque to pray after they had found enough. I continued to sit there and eat to lighten the load in my backpack. The road was unchanged. I continued.

I came across two stands at the opposite side of the road, and I headed over to see what I could buy for something to eat; plus, I needed water. I asked the person over there what they were cooking, and it turned out to be corn on the cob. 'I will have one of those. Thanks,' I said, pointing to the corn on the cob, a healthy and delicious snack. There was no water there.

Energy levels retained, I cycled and noticed a car and a person returning ever so hastily from across the road from another food place. As I was passing, the person was returning. They were of clean appearance, I not so much; I had been cycling for six or seven days straight, no wash. We chatted. I was heading to Erzurum like they were. I was thinking, *Nice one, free lift*. I should have listened. They were from east Turkey and were travelling from Austria. I removed the two wheels from the bicycle. And for the first time, I realised that the bicycle can be transported in a normal-sized car; in I got. It was a clean car and clean person. I was a dirty person—comfortable though.

'You know, this is too comfortable for myself. This is not how I travel,' I said.

'Sometimes it is okay to travel in comfort,' they replied. I supposed they were right. I deserved somewhat of a break.

We drove several hundred kilometres before we had to stop for fuel. Suddenly, I had to take money out of my account to pay. As I said, I should have listened. 'We share the costs.' This was not part of my plan. I had to think about it as *Do I really want to pay for this transport?* At least it was not public transport.

When getting the Turkish lira, I only withdrew half of what they expected. 'Wait until the tank is done. Then you fill up. Then I fill up,' I said.

We continued on the road for another few hours before I had to pay for a hotel in Amasya, a beautiful city surrounded by the mountains. Again, I had to pay for the both of us. I was raging a wee bit. It cost less than twenty pound sterling each, breakfast included, all you can eat. I did take advantage of it, like this person had of me and my card. It was a great start to the day. I ate until I was full.

That night, I had a great sleep on a bed, first one in a while. Unfortunately, my sleep was cut short after a knock on the door, rather early for breakfast. This was had on the terrace with a view of the Amasya Castle. It was a nice place but wasn't worth the exploration; you could see it all from the view of your seat. Breakfast was had, and it was time for the weekly shower and change of clothes—the travelling lifestyle for me. No need to shower every day, especially as you travel and don't have the facilities. You are not out to impress—well, I was not.

Into the car we went in search of the city of Erzurum, another five hundred kilometres to go. The sights along the way were powerful. Multiple layers of sand and rock were on show from the mountains. The landscape was forever changing; we really were going east. There were plenty of hills, mountains, and stones. We quickly stopped for food. I only had five Turkish lira, they offered the other five, and we ate. I ate until my heart and belly were content, and then we were back on the road again.

One hundred kilometres later, we arrived in Erzurum. This person was good enough compared with others I had taken lifts from. They were sound enough. We amicably shook hands, and away I went. 'Where will you sleep tonight?' they asked.

'I will think about that when the time is right,' I said.

They went towards the Iranian border. I went to find Wi-Fi in the city of Erzurum and to scope it out slightly, though it was three o'clock in the afternoon. I thought I would try to find a place to stay as it can be hard to find a place to camp in the city, though not always. But first, Wi-Fi. I locked up my bicycle on the main street. I would have no problem locating it when I returned. I headed down a side street and saw many places with Internet facilities but no Wi-Fi, only paid computers. What sort of city was this? Then it struck me; I was left off at a university—students.

I continued heading down the street until I got to a functioning street with many watering holes. I saw one watering hole and headed down a set of stairs to use the Wi-Fi. Everything was okay; I can use. I was asked if I would like a drink from one of the bartenders. 'No thank you,' I replied.

I was in the watering hole to use the Wi-Fi only to transfer money from my student overdraft. I was asked again if I would like a drink. 'No', I replied. I was asked a third time, and I gave in. They filled me like a balloon with jars of water.

The next day, I awakened in a hospital, not having any recollection of what happened the previous night. I guess I found my place to stay that night. I stayed in the hospital for as long as possible, eventually being ushered out of the complex. I walked to an empty room and helped myself to a bed. I slept until about four o'clock in the afternoon. I had a shower and made my way out of the complex through the car park. I decided not to check out as I was afraid there may be a bill to be paid.

I headed out not knowing where I was. I was in the middle of nowhere. This was almost desert land. It was like something out of Vice City, the PlayStation game. Just waking up in the middle of nowhere, in the desert, in a hospital, then continuing where you woke up.

I asked a group of people if they knew how to get back to the city centre; they brought me to the bus, and towards the centre we went. I was fragile that afternoon. They asked if I wanted food or if I was hungry. 'I could eat,' I replied. They brought me to this delicious kebab hut which seemed like the most delicious kebab I had ever eaten.

Afterwards, we split, hands were shook, and off to the watering hole across the street I went to pick up the rest of my belongings from the night before—most notably a laptop—and to possibly apologise for my actions from the night before but I was sure that I had not done anything too extreme. I headed across the road with a water in hand. One of the owners, managers, or their mates spotted me as I was crossing. They spoke in Turkish, and I didn't understand but knew. They mentioned the night before. 'Why do you think I am here?' I responded.

I headed into the watering hole and got smiley faces from all the staff. I was asked into the office, where there was a group of six. I was not sure what role each of them played, but surely, that was not my business.

Henchmen, I was thinking. I was offered a tea, and the owner slid over a piece of paper that said '400 lira'. I looked at it and was baffled; there was no chance that much water was drank the previous night. Then some food arrived, spicy bread; it looked delicious. One of the people offered me a slice, and I accepted. It was tasty. I was offered another. I rejected the third.

The bartender from the night before came into the office, and I followed them to the computer, where we had a digital conversation using Google Translate. One by one, we input our phrases and let the translator do the work. Eventually, I put in the phrase 'Can I work off the bill?' At this stage, another manager came through to respond to the question with 'Have this as a gift.' All right then, all was well!

I picked up my backpack, and away I went, wondering where my laptop was. The bartender had said that the police had taken it. I was confused as why on earth would the police have it? I was directed to the police station, which was quite busy for a Sunday evening. I spoke to the guard out front who had an automatic machine gun. I thought they might know something—no. I was able to translate my story using my hand language and signals; they understood but did not know where the laptop was.

I headed in and waited patiently until the officer at the desk was finished with their business. The police officer asked what the problem was. In broken english, a conversation was had. They understood my problem and asked me to take a seat. I waited patiently for the correct officer to speak, a few stopped over for a chat as they were bewildered about why I was there. A tea was offered, and I accepted. I continued to wait. I decided to ask the first police person what was happening—you know, what the story was. They told me an english-speaking officer was on their way. Excellent.

In a matter of time, the police person showed up and was directed towards me. One wrote; the other translated. The police person understood the situation. At this stage, it was getting late. They asked about the bicycle, the brand, the model number, and the colour, but this was not lost; this should still be on the high street. Eventually, they decided to make calls to other stations in the neighbourhood.

They called the hospital from the night before, and the laptop was located. I was about to leave when the Turkish police person said that they would drive me there.

Sweet, it saved me from cycling. I said this before—this place was out of the way.

Twenty minutes later, we arrived. We headed in, I kept my head down as much as possible, and we headed into the police station within the complex. Words were exchanged between the police people, I assumed about the situation. Hands were shook. A short time passed, and the head police person took out a key, opened the top drawer, and took out the laptop. I was relieved the device I had been using to communicate had been returned. Hooray! There was no charger or bag though, just the important part.

The police people were heading back to the station, but they wanted to see the bicycle or to see if I remembered where I parked it. Success. The bicycle was located easily. It was only on its side, still complete, with both wheels attached along with the speedometer and lights. Erzurum was the friendliest place in Turkey and the coldest.

That night, I felt the chills of the winter temperature. I decided to find a budget hotel for the night. I cycled up the high street, coming to a sign pointing to a hotel up a side street. I headed in. 'How much for a room, one person, one night?' I asked.

'Sixty-five lira', replied the attendant.

'No thank you,' I replied.

'Fifty lira', they responded.

'That will do rightly,' I replied.

That was less than fifteen pound sterling. Checkout was at midday, breakfast included—and Wi-Fi. I didn't even see the room or ask anything. That night, I needed a warm place to sleep after my ordeal. I headed upstairs to the room, opened the door, and lay on the double bed all to myself. En suite, television, and table—you didn't get that when you camp in the wild.

I dropped off my backpack and went into Erzurum in search of food and water. I decided to call into the watering hole from the night before for a final time to see if my charger was there. I arrived, and I was not allowed past the stairwell. A translator was pulled out, and a conversation was had. No charger though.

That day, I had been feeling fragile, and all I wanted was a drink of Fanta. I headed to the shop and picked up a drink, something to munch, and a few kebabs. Compared with back home, kebabs abroad were nothing like those available from the 'Authentic Turkish Restaurant'. I think they actually use real meat abroad though I could be wrong! Food in hand, I returned to the hotel to eat, use the Internet, and have a good uninterrupted sleep in the heat. Warmth was what I needed that night.

The next morning, I awakened at half past eleven and headed down for breakfast, taking full advantage of what was on offer—no cereal and milk, though mainly a selection of breads, meats, eggs, jams, and honey. That afternoon, I was ready to head to the Iranian consulate to get my visa or at least one step closer. I headed off on my bicycle and went down the hill in the pouring rain to the building. I found the consulate without bother as I had asked the manager where it was; it was basically down the road, last left turn past the police station and straight ahead. I found the building as there was an Iranian flag outside; this was the only indicator. I thought these buildings were supposed to be special. But another country's consulate, why would it be special? I headed in, I took a seat, I was called forwards, and I filled out a form and returned it. I needed two passport photographs and forty euros for the visa.

Down the road I walked with bicycle in hand. I stopped and had a chat with a Turkish person drinking a glass of water outside their shop, and they offered me one. We talked and drank. Hands were shook, and away I went towards a photograph shop.

As I continued, I passed a ginger person sitting at the side of the road; they looked out of place, as did I. The person was layered up with coating to protect themselves from the harsh coldness of Erzurum. I decided to head back and talk to them; maybe they were from Ireland. No, they were from Germany and travelling without money. They could speak english very well. They were also heading to Iran but were having difficulty attaining their visa. I brought them back to the hotel lobby as I thought I could help them in attaining their visa. We were able to use my laptop as you can apply for the visa online or at least get one step closer to applying. Time passed, and the form had been submitted along with a letter explaining the purpose of travel. Hopefully, they were able to help them on their quest to get to Jerusalem to pray. Walking down the road, we split, them in search of food in a nearby village, I to find passport photographs. Hands were shook, and away we went.

I asked a Turkish person if they knew where I could find photographs, and they pointed across the street and down the road about twenty metres. I should really open my eyes a little wider. I headed over and into the shop. A photograph was taken, and I continued to wait until I was directed downstairs where I was given six photographs in a pouch. The person directed me to go. I waited around, but they did not ask for payment— sound person.

Next on my agenda was to head to a bank to pay the forty-euro visa charge and return the receipt to the consulate. Why euro though? Better exchange rate maybe. I headed into the bank, took a number, and waited until I was called. Eventually, after about an hour, I was served, though not quite. When I tried to pay with my debit card, there were two problems: I cannot pay with card and cannot convert here. I must go to another bank. Surely, any bank should be able to convert money—no, not here.

I headed back to the consulate to see if they accepted another currency. They were not happy to see me. The answer was no. I headed back to the hotel for a quick nap, which took longer than planned. Luckily, though, the banks shut at one o'clock in the afternoon. I headed around to another bank to get the money changed into euro and was successful. Now I had to go back to the first bank to pay for the visa.

As I was waiting in line, I had a laugh with a Turkish person there who was finding it funny how the number system skipped about; there was no logic. When it was my turn, the request was processed. By the time I returned to the consulate, the place had shut for the day. It would have to wait until morning. Energy levels falling, I returned to the hotel for Internet and to recuperate.

The next morning, I awakened around breakfast time and headed to the consulate. I pressed the buzzer to the door with no answer. The security guard told me to push it for longer—no answer. Eventually, a person left the building. This was my chance, and I headed in. I took a seat and waited. I was called forwards, the receipt was handed over, and now all I had to do was wait for my visa. Half an hour later, I had my visa in hand, though I noticed it was only valid for thirty days. How was I to get my next visa and cycle through Iran within thirty days? It was not their problem. There was nothing I can do there but plan my journey through Iran. I returned to the hotel.

For the last few days, I was not feeling quite right. I decided to get yet another night in the hotel, very convenient, but I was not ready or fit to leave. Saturday's escapades really took it out of me. Even walking up three flights of stairs was a chore. The rest of the day, I kept myself warm and connected to the Wi-Fi. I picked up supplies for the next few days. I hibernated for a while before feeling fit again.

On the day I decided to leave, I headed along the high street, looking for warmer clothing to wear. I saw a person selling socks. I chatted with them to see what else they had; there was nothing really but socks and hats. I left with several pairs of socks, a decent winter hat, and a pair of gloves, all for twenty Turkish lira. We headed to a shop a few doors down to use a translator. They now understood that I was looking to buy clothes for winter. They brought me to a shop where I was able to buy a heavy woollen jumper for twenty Turkish lira. It would do the job.

Next to look for was a pair of trainers as my sandals were lost last weekend. We headed to a shop, but all the products were branded and out of my price range. I saw a box with bargain shoes, thirty Turkish lira for a pair of non-laced Adidas trainers; it must be a new design—or counterfeit.

They fitted and would do the job for cycling. Shopping done, it was now time to return to the hotel to fix a puncture and be on the road once again towards the next place on my travels, Doğubayazit.

I had several stops in between, with many unknown places. That week, I had not been buying bottled water that was on sale at the hotel. I was just refilling my Fanta bottle and drinking the tap water. That week, my stomach had been turned inside out. I was unsure whether this was due to the hotel's water or the water I had last weekend. I found it strange that the only item in the hotel's fridge was bottled water, nothing else. Surely if the water was safe to wash your face, shave, and clean, it should be safe to drink? Definitely not.

I set off on my travels, taking my time with the cycling. I saw children playing in the distance, and they noticed me. 'Hello, hello, hello!' the three of them shouted at me from the distance. I waved and continued to cycle, but they were coming over. I decided to stop as it had been a steady incline out of Erzurum, and I was in need of a drink of water. The children came over to me. I had nothing to give but some shampoo. They were happy enough; it was better than nothing, I supposed. They even offered me a glass of water, and I accepted. It was powerful. I had no Turkish lira, only pound sterling. There were three of them, and they were not brothers. Had I given them a twenty-pound note, how would it have been split? Would it have been split? Which one would I have given it to? I did ponder this sometime before departing. I couldn't. Who knew what would happen?

Off I went down the road to Doğubayazit. This was my first day back to cycling after my slight ailment. I probably should have stayed another night, but I was wrapped up warm and prepared. I cycled eighty kilometres, fifty miles, before deciding to rest for the night in the place of Horasan. I took advice from the ginger traveller, which was to knock on three doors and see if someone can help you. My case was to see if there was somewhere safe to place a tent for the night. *Door one, here I go.* They were busy.

At door two, they decided to ask another family across the yard. The head of the house came out. We chatted. I asked if I could place the tent beside a large stack of hay, and we headed over.

They were baffled. They told me of the hotels in the centre. I rubbed my thumb and index finger together to show money. Yes, I had previously stayed in a hotel for the week, but that was different. 'No para', they said, meaning 'no money'. I argued—well, not that I argued. I said hotels equal money. I was happy to place my tent there. Then they mentioned a taxi. Again, I showed my thumb and index finger; plus, I had a bicycle.

I was directed towards a path along with a family member. They headed off, returned with their car, and drove me to the city, with bicycle in the back, of course. When I put on my seat belt, they laughed. We headed to a teahouse. I was offered tea and food. I accepted as I was famished from the afternoon of cycling. I say 'teahouse' as I had no other name for it, but it had tea. Time passed, chat was had, translator was used, and it looked like I was to be camping somewhere in town. They had asked if I had tried the police or the hospital. They called the police to see if there was a bed available—no luck.

Eventually, we found that a room was available above the teahouse. I was amazed. The person was right, no money indeed. I was shown to the room. I locked the door and headed for sleep. Turkish people were a friendly race, or maybe people were, the right people.

That morning, I awoke at six o'clock to vacate the room. Tea was had in the teahouse. The person even gave me a bag of cucumbers for the road. I had never thought of vegetable sandwiches before. I had been eating meat with every meal, more or less. This was a way forwards as processed meat was not really meat at all. We headed out the front, and I was ready to go.

The night before, I was asked if I was in town for the sacrifice and that I should stay. I had no idea what they were talking about. Was I to be the sacrifice? Surely not and I was not staying around to find out.

Off towards Ağrı I went, one hundred kilometres. Starting at six o'clock, I could be done in a day with no problems, though I hadn't taken into consideration the condition of the route. I set off down the road, cycling calmly. The sun was just coming up; the temperature was reminiscent of an October in the North of Ireland. Hats and face warmers were on; they really did help keep me at a reasonable temperature. The road was not too bad; it was quiet, not a lot of traffic.

After fifteen kilometres, I decided to take a break. I saw some beautiful-looking gorges that would make for a good photograph, very eastern. I decided to take out my laptop to take a few photographs.

As I was sitting at the side of the road, a BMW motorbike was slowly approaching, and it stopped. A person slowly got off their motorbike; they were very well prepared. Their motorbike was carrying a heavy load, though they looked comfortable. We talked. They had biked from Japan to as far as the Netherlands or bought the motorbike in the Netherlands and were on their way back to Japan, doing a loop; they had many badges on their motorbike. Before they went, they gave me some nugget. I gave them some pistachio nuts that I was eating. We ate a little before heading off down the road. They were quicker off the mark, being on a motorbike.

I, on the bicycle, composed myself before I was ready to get back on the road. I cycled for several kilometres before passing a field close to a house where I could see a cow being suspended in the air by the front of a tractor as a sacrifice to Allah.

It was halal meat in the making. They called me to come over from the road, and I was offered a cup of tea and a seat. I saw the skinned cow's head on the floor, which the dog was playing with, and the people in the background cutting meat off the cow. Meat was brought over, and I was invited over to eat with the family. This was a real breakfast to start me off for the day. I had two portions before setting off on the bicycle.

A few kilometres later, I passed another family celebrating, but I did not stop; I had my feast. There were some children at the side of the road, and I did not stop; stones were thrown towards me. Cheeky children, or maybe I was the one who was cheeky for not stopping. I had nothing to give them apart from myself, which would be enough, but I didn't feel like stopping.

I set off up a mountain. When I reached the top, I took a break to admire the view. I was sitting at the side of the road, drinking glasses of water, eating nuts, half-heartedly throwing my thumb out to the passing trucks. Two trucks were approaching. The first driver did not acknowledge me. The second truck pulled in and stopped. Oh, happy days. I spoke to the driver. I mentioned the place Ağrı, and they were going that way. In I bounced. Names were exchanged and forgotten. We set off down the road that would take me towards Iran. After Ağrı, I would go to Doğubayazit and stay the night, crossing the border on Monday—a full day to start the visa.

We set off on the road, only for the truck to begin to fail several kilometres later. The driver got out of the cabin, and then I got out a short while later to see what the problem was. There was a problem with the fuel line unfortunately. I had no fuel for the lorry, only food, my fuel. The driver opened up a cupboard and removed a siphon to extract the fuel from the secondary tank. Pump, pump! It was good to go. We set off once more.

I was very comfortable. I had gotten used to getting dropped off in an unknown location. It no longer scared or bothered me as I can always find a way. I was free from that burden. The driver offered me a glass of water, and I accepted. They spoke Turkish. We were able to communicate using my sketchpad—well, I understood. We passed through Ağrı; I stayed put.

Before the place of Taslicay, the truck began to have trouble. Out we got to have a look, and it was a similar problem with the fuel and oil. After a while, I headed off into the town to see what was about and to see about using Internet facilities. While there, I chatted with a friend who mentioned Dubai as a place of refuge from the harsh coldness of winter. As I was at the Internet station, I was able to transfer money from my student overdraft onto my debit card to withdraw from the cash machine as I thought the driver needed money for petrol.

I returned to the truck, and we headed over to the petrol station with a jerrycan to fill up, enough to get the truck going. By this stage, it was late in the night, and there was no sign of the driver starting the engine—well, once to see if it was working. It was raining outside; they offered me the second bunk in their truck, and I accepted as it was lashing outside. I slept the night away.

In the morning, we headed towards Doğubayazit. Here, the driver was able to check in with their employer. At this stage, I was ready to go into Iran. But there was something not quite right. It turned out the driver was heading to Tehran. I may as well take a lift with them, but it wasn't quite like that. I wanted to stay the night in Doğubayazit and cross the border in the morning. I would now be crossing in a free lift. There was no problem about that.

When the driver was seeing their manager, I was unable to produce the receipt that was used to pay for the petrol unfortunately. They might be losing out on money. What a pity. They were a sound person.

Anyway, we headed off to the border. About one hundred trucks were all waiting to cross. We parked up, and the driver and I headed into the middle of border patrol. I wasn't quite sure why, but it was to return the money for the petrol. When we were there, one of the border patrol said that I was not allowed to cross with the driver. I must travel through myself. By the time we had returned to the truck, I could see a pulley strap blowing in the wind, and I immediately knew what had happened. Someone had stolen my bicycle. I was correct.

Luckily, I kept the spare wheel in the cabin to help with the storage. The driver and I headed to the border police who had a look about the area which was kind of like slums—dry slums as the weather was reasonably settled at the time. They were unable to help. The army were called, and an hour later, the bicycle was retrieved. I assumed they were able to search the area properly. I was not sure what happened to the person or people who stole it. I believe it was the border children.

As I was waiting, I headed off to the shop to pick up some comfort food as I couldn't believe that I had had my bicycle stolen. When I returned there, I could see my bicycle and thanked all those who were able to help, and I even took a photograph with the army. Good people. At the border, a person outside in a car asked to see my passport—slim chance, they would have driven away with it. It would have been a funny story to tell!

As I was not able to cross the border in the truck, we had to part ways. Another person had translated for the driver that I was to cross the border, camp several kilometres along the road, and hop back in the cabin. I slept on the Turkish border as I wanted to cross the patrol after the clock had struck midnight. Then I would get the full thirty-day visa in the Islamic Republic of Iran.

Instead of following the driver's instructions, I decided to wait at the Turkey-Iran border, crossing the next day as then I would have the full thirty-day visa. I asked the police if I could place my tent until the end of the day. I was directed to a yard where I could set up camp for the night. I set up the tent as this would give me time to sleep in my temporary home before setting off into the unknown country of the Islamic Republic of Iran.

As I was lying in the tent, I was keeping my eye on the passing trucks that were going through customs as I really needed this lift to Tehran seven hundred kilometres as this would give me a brave start into the country. Had I been cycling, it would have taken me, at the most, ten days to get to the capital, Tehran. It would be constant cycling and sleeping, time wasted in my opinion as you can enjoy the view as easily as a passenger.

Time passed. Time to cross the border. I wasn't quite ready yet as I still had to find the driver who would take me all those kilometres in the comfort of the lorry and at a cost that was never mentioned. They were a good person, like no other Turkish driver I had met. They had plenty of craic and asked nothing from me, good person.

I awoke, and it was a new day. Instead of crossing straight away, I decided to have a check of the lorries to see if I could see the lorry I had been in. When I peered out the tent, I noticed two Mercedes lorries that were carrying several Caterpillar diggers, heavy machinery.

It wasn't easy to forget; they were massive mechanical machines that were several trucks in front of the driver.

I continued to wait. I had several glasses of water while I waited. Still, no luck; time passed. I had another look down the line of lorries—still nothing. Time did not stop. I continued to wait until the sun was coming up before I crossed into the Islamic Republic. I had tried several entrances before being directed to the correct entrance, which felt like a prison.

As I crossed, there was a heightened level of security compared with the other borders that I had crossed. There were several guards on either side, army people patrolling at each side, and several checks beforehand. I was literally in a hurry. I wanted to see if my lift was still there somewhere over the border, but the border patrol did not understand this. Maybe I was the reason and my Irish passport, seeing as it was in a different language, though speed and efficiency was not part of their game; one finger typing should never be acceptable, though maybe this was what I should expect in the Islamic Republic. I knew nothing of the country apart from the fact that Islam was the chosen religion of the masses. I waited patiently with the bicycle in hand until I was served, and my passport was returned.

What was I doing here? Should I be here? Was I allowed to be here? Would I survive in this country? Would I be safe?

To be continued.